August 2014

A Child of the Sun

For Marilyn

Remembering our expedition
to Pacifica & Funston Park,
And your wonderful hospitality to me
— and to Becca!

To be continued...

Love,
Pierce

A CHILD OF THE SUN

Pierce Butler

Beech Hill Publishing Company
Mount Desert, Maine

BEECH HILL PUBLISHING COMPANY
Mount Desert, Maine 04660

www.beechhillpublishingcompany.com

ISBN: 978-0-9908200-8-6

Printed on acid-free paper in the United States of America

Cover design by Pamela Trush
www.delaney-designs.com

For Susan Holbert
unstinting giver
wise counsellor
true companion

For my friends at Camp Caravan
whose work and wisdom are also here

But I tell you, my Lord fool,
Out of this nettle, danger, we pluck this flower, safety.

HENRY IV, PART I

Faith of consciousness is freedom
Faith of feeling is weakness
Faith of body is stupidity.

Love of consciousness evokes the same in response
Love of feeling evokes the opposite
Love of body depends only on type and polarity.

Hope of consciousness is strength
Hope of feeling is slavery
Hope of body is disease.

G. I. Gurdjieff
ALL AND EVERYTHING

Prefatory Note

A CHILD OF THE SUN is a novel based on the writer Katherine Mansfield's time at the Institute for the Harmonious Development of Man (aka the Prieuré), a school established in 1921 by George Ivanovich Gurdjieff to provide practical training in esoteric discipline. The novel arose from my love for KM's writing and for Mr Gurdjieff's teaching, which I have studied and practiced for more than 30 years.

I chose to write primarily in the voice of KM's journal, which leaves off when she departs Paris for the Prieuré in September, 1922. In this journal, KM frequently gave titles to her entries, drafted her letters, and wrote of herself in the third person, and I have adopted these conventions. I've drawn on the many accounts of life at the Prieuré, but my main sources of inspiration are the published journal and KM's letters to her husband, John Middleton Murray (JMM). My hope is to give an imaginative account of KM's inner life during her last three months, as she might have written it herself, had she been inclined, with the detachment and honesty of the journal. KM was a sensitive young woman who was drawn to Gurdjieff's teaching, experienced his compassion, and faced death with great courage and attention.

A few words about the originals of my characters. Growing up literary in an upper middle-class family in distant New Zealand, Katherine Mansfield longed for London, the center of the literary universe. In many respects she was the black sheep of her family, and though she succeeded in persuading her parents to allow her to pursue a literary career far from home, her personal behavior brought about a permanent estrangement. KM was a brilliant conversationalist who delighted in malicious wit, a writer with an exquisite sense of form who sometimes sacrificed honesty for aesthetic effect, and a freethinking woman whose bold exploration of her sexuality resulted in a number of liaisons that even her bohemian circle regarded as indiscreet. In 1922, she was on the verge of literary celebrity. She was the friend of Virginia Woolf and D. H. Lawrence, and her remarkable stories were changing the way people thought about the form. But she was also deeply unhappy in her marriage to Murry—and she was dying of tuberculosis. When she abandoned the nomadic life of an invalid in search of the ideal climate and put herself in the hands of Gurdjieff, she was taking a step into the unknown.

A spiritual seeker of Greek and Armenian parentage, G. I. Gurdjieff had traveled extensively among esoteric communities in the East, fled the Revolution in Russia, and brought to France and England an eclectic teaching that combined Christian spirituality with Sufi mysticism. He was little known in the West, but he was preceded by the Russian mathematician P. D. Ouspensky whose writing introduced KM to Gurdjieff's ideas. The Gurdjieff Institute occupied the Prieuré de Basse Loges, a magnificent chateau in the woods of Fontainebleau that had once been the residence of Mme. de Maintenon. His work at the Prieuré had attracted the attention of many writers and artists, among them Alfred Orage, editor of *The New Age*, who had published KM's early work and encouraged her interest in Gurdjieff.

A CHILD OF THE SUN is a work of fiction. The story is grounded in the historical record, except in regard to the character of Patrick whose relationship with KM is purely fiction. Anyone who is familiar with the history of the Prieuré will recognize Fritz Peters in the character of Patrick—and will know that Peters was a child at the Prieuré two years after KM's sojourn there. I created this fictional relationship to give expression to the longing for a child that appears so frequently in KM's published journal and letters. The child that Fritz Peters was at the Prieuré is also close to my heart, and the character of Patrick gave me the opportunity to explore his predicament, as well as the nature of Gurdjieff's relationships with the children and adults of the Prieuré.

In order to go to the Prieuré, KM had to put aside the reservations of her husband and literary friends. She was accompanied by her friend Ida Baker, aka Lesley Moore (LM), who had her own apprehensions about the place and did not stay, although she remained in France in order to be close at hand. Seen from the perspective of her writing, KM's life is a going-forth from a place of innocence and certainty, a solitary passage through an inhospitable landscape, and—as the cloud of her illness increasingly darkens the horizon—a destination that seems to offer little comfort. But her time with Gurdjieff is an episode that, like the finely crafted end of a meandering story, gives form and meaning to what has gone before.

—Pierce Butler

JMM

My late wife Katherine Mansfield Murry entered the Gurdjieff Institute at Fontainebleau on 16th October, 1922. Less than three months later, on 9th January, 1923, she died there. She had convinced herself that the tuberculosis affecting her lungs had an underlying spiritual or psychological cause; if she could address herself to this underlying cause, under the direction of Gurdjieff, her health would improve of its own accord. She reached this conclusion as a result of the failure of an equally dubious medical treatment to alleviate her condition. Her desire to be well was such that she could not accept the limitations imposed upon her by her illness, and so she must seek a spiritual technique that would enable her to ignore it. I could not share her hope of a medical miracle, but I was obliged to behave as if I did, in order to avoid the charge of giving her up for dead. Neither could I share the faith she placed in spiritual transformation as a way to transcend her illness. On this matter I was unable to dissemble, and it produced a estrangement between us. For the first time since we had known each other, there was a real parting of the ways.

In June, 1921, Katherine and I settled into the Chalet des Sapins in Montana-sur-Sierre in the Valais. The clear dry air of the mountains seemed to work its magic. She was at peace and working well. We wrote all morning and most of the afternoon; the evenings we spent together. Katherine produced some of her best stories during her time at Sierre. She was following a real regimen for the first time since she became ill, and there is no doubt in my mind that the condition of her lungs was much improved by it.

But it was as though her very happiness proved her undoing. To be happy with me made her long to be well so that we could enjoy each other all the more. She felt that I was making a great sacrifice just to be with her in Sierre, when the truth was that I could have desired nothing more. And she reproached herself constantly for idleness, which in reality was simply the exhaustion that

1

follows intense creative work, exacerbated by her physical weakness. The result was that she began to cast about for a miracle and she fixed upon the Manoukhin treatment, which involves irradiation of the spleen, as her last chance for full and complete recovery.

At this critical moment there occurred another event that contributed to her restlessness: A. R. Orage sent me a book called *Cosmic Anatomy* for review. It was a book of occult doctrines, the sort of thing for which I felt little sympathy, and I'm sure I gave it short shrift. To this day I cannot understand his sending the book to me. But perhaps there was already something disingenuous in this, perhaps he intended the book for Katherine from the first, realizing that in her fragile state of body and mind she would be particularly susceptible to the ideas it contained. At any rate, into Katherine's hands it fell, and she drank it in as a man dying of thirst might swallow tainted water. I credit this book with setting her feet upon the path that led to Fontainebleau, a path upon which I could not accompany her.

In January, 1922, Katherine and her companion Ida Moore left Sierre for Paris, where Katherine was to see Dr. Manoukhin. My greatest regret is that I did not more resolutely oppose this journey. To my way of thinking, Katherine was abandoning the mountains and putting at risk the gains she had made there, as well as the peace and quiet that had enabled her to produce some of her best work—for the sake of a mirage. I could not believe in the possibility of a miracle, but to my sorrow I was unable to tell her so, in spite of my foreboding. I felt that my concern for her health was of no help to her and that my lack of sympathy with her spiritual aspirations was simply exasperating.

After she had seen Manoukhin, she decided to begin the treatments immediately. In February I joined her in Paris. In giving up the Chalet, I felt that I had stepped outside the magic circle we had created for ourselves and put us at the mercy of the larger world with all its perils and accidents. If we could remain together and resolve to live only for each other, all might yet be well. At very least, Katherine's life might have been considerably prolonged. We had shared a dream of a rural sanctuary somewhere in the south of England, to be named The Heron in memory of her brother, Leslie Heron Beauchamp, who had died in the War. There we would write and live for ourselves alone, in close contact with the land and with all the living things of the countryside that Katherine so loved. Though we had often been separated by Katherine's quest for health and my editorial responsibilities, this dream remained alive, a golden thread that was eventually to lead us home. But with the advent of *Cosmic Anatomy*, the thread was severed. It was as though Katherine abandoned the promise of The Heron for a supra-terrestrial paradise. Now her eyes seemed to look beyond this world; if there was desire in them, it was desire for the void, for forgetfulness, for self-annihilation.

At first the Manoukhin treatments seemed to produce a beneficial effect. Katherine wrote to Ida in London that she felt the disease of her lungs to have been arrested and that her heart would soon recover. In June we returned to the mountains, and what I had feared came to pass. For Katherine the journey was debilitating in the extreme; she arrived in Randogne more dead than alive. Soon she was obliged to send for Ida and to move to the Hotel Chateau Belle Vue in Sierre, where Ida looked after her. The dream of The Heron was dead; we were never again to sleep together under the same roof.

How to describe my state of being at this time? It was utter prostration, both physical and emotional. The last few months had brought me to the limit of my capacity to bear the spectacle of Katherine's illness. To feel those burning eyes upon me, to hear that cough, to lie awake beside her knowing she too was awake and suffering—and to be quite unable to help. My misery merely irritated her, and so I was obliged to remove myself from her sight. In my mind I aspired to share her pain, but in reality I could not even share what remained of her life. If by an effort of will I could have believed in what she called "the ideas," if I could have shared her striving for the Beyond—or at least acknowledged the efficacy of such a striving for one in her predicament—I would have done so. But I could not change my nature to accommodate her need, no matter how much I desired it. I had been driven back upon my last defense, and I clung to the Mind, to the power of reason to make reasonable choices, in the face of what I perceived as the vast bottomless pit of the occult.

In August Katherine wrote me a farewell letter that was found among her papers after her death. Her parting words: "In spite of everything—how happy we have been! I feel no two lovers have walked the earth more joyfully—in spite of all." She also made a will, which was witnessed by two of the hotel staff. In her desperate state of mind she desired me to burn as much of her writings as possible, a request with which I have been unable to comply. On the 16th her restless spirit dictated another removal, this time to London, ostensibly to consult Dr. Sorapure, for whom she had a great regard, about the condition of her heart. But I was aware that the seed planted by *Cosmic Anatomy* had begun to bear fruit. Katherine had been in correspondence with Orage, and it was to Orage that she was going. She had all but lost hope in medicine and was turning toward "the ideas" for solace.

In London our separation continued, though we lived next door to each other in Pond Street. Katherine was quickly drawn into a circle, of which Orage was a member, surrounding P. D. Ouspensky, and since I could not join her without doing violence to my sense of intellectual integrity, I was increasingly shut out of her life—while she continued to believe that if only I were to hear Ouspensky or to talk to Orage, the impediment to my participation in her all-consuming interest would be miraculously removed and we would find ourselves again quite at one. I might have spoken to Orage, if only to ask what sort of people Katherine had fallen in with. But we had been rivals in the past, I had virtually stolen Katherine away from New Age, the weekly he still edited, and I feared that he would lord it over me in my misfortune. As for Ouspensky I knew only that he was a lecturer on occult subjects who had escaped the Revolution in Russia by the skin of his teeth, and it was more than my life was worth to feign an interest in his particular brand of mysticism, even for the sake of being better enabled to disagree with my wife.

Behind Orage and Ouspensky lurked the shadowy figure of George Ivanovich Gurdjieff. History has assigned to Gurdjieff his place, and a most ambiguous one it is. But what was known of him at the time, apart from the gnomic utterances of Ouspensky? Next to nothing. He had been wandering around the near East for years, gathering wisdom from dervishes and cowherds, he had brought his mission to Russia, where he emerged miraculously unscathed from the Revolution, and he had made his way to Paris and set up shop in his apartment. This sort of thing was outside the realm of my experience. What was I to say to Katherine? It is obvious to me now that it was the spiritual vacuum created by the war that allowed such fellows to peddle their questionable wares. But at the time I experienced a sort of moral paralysis. I did not choose to know how Katherine's time was spent, and for her part she did not tell me all that she was thinking as before, no doubt because she was too well aware of my lack of sympathy.

In September I removed to Selsfield, and on the 27th I received a letter from Katherine informing me that she was going to Paris to resume the Manoukhin treatments. I hastened back to town, and there ensued yet another parting, which she likened to that of a brother and sister who are not particularly fond of each other. The name of Gurdjieff was not mentioned by either of us, but I knew that once in Paris she would find a way of going to him. I was powerless to intervene. For my part the attrition of so many partings had simply rendered me numb; this one did not materially add to my sum of grief. And yet it seems to me now that Katherine's aloofness communicated a chill. Away with song and laughter, she seemed to say, away with garden parties and literary magazines and firelight trysts. Away with cottages in the country, with the speaking silence of work, with a shared glance and the knowledge of sympathy. Welcome, cold waste of stars, welcome, cold, cold grave.

All of this happened a long time ago. It seems to me that I have lived my life twice over since those painful days. I am an old man now, and I have worn out all my illusions.

But Katie, if only we had not left Sierre. One more book, containing only the best. It was already planned, it was waiting in the wings, lacking only patience to bring it to birth. The world will never see it now. You told me that you were going to Fontainebleau to undertake the Work. I have never understood what you meant. What work, what real work, the vision of which first drew us together, what work that will survive could you possibly have done with Gurdjieff?

HOPE

KM

3 October

Arrived Paris. Took rooms in the Select, Place de la Sorbonne. What is my state? Indifference? Not that.   I am tired, tired to the death. Tired of departure, tired of arrival, tired of living in a virtual strait-jacket of ill-health as I have done for the past five years. "That I have borne and yet must bear..." The life of an invalid has made me intolerable to myself and to those around me. Only LM is capable of putting up with me, and she does it by means of a sort of transubstantiation of emotion, of enmity into love, an alchemy that baffles me and leaves her looking pale and sleepless. To be separated from Jack. But what was our life together? What had it become? He was tender when he remembered to be, when his own ailments allowed him a reprieve. (How should I sit still under my burden when Jack, hale and hearty, is driven to distraction by the boils on his neck? I must.) His most precious dream was of a life with me, freed from all constraint of circumstance or ill-health. But that is all we had of such a life: a dream. And I had begun to wonder if it was really a shared dream. The child, for example, our child, who was to be such a large part of that life. Jack was worried sick about my ability to bear a child. Would my constitution be able to stand it? But really! Time and time again I found myself apologizing to him for the intrusion of "our" child upon this life he wanted for us. That was before it became manifestly clear to me that we would never have children, would never lie like the parents of the race looking up at the innumerable stars of the sky while our own little star, flesh of our flesh, lay between us...

A dream is not enough when one must live day by day with the reality of its frustration. Why have I gone away from Jack? Because we simply cannot go on like this, one healthy, the other an invalid, both ailing in spirit. Because I have not come to myself. It is nonsense to believe that my problem is purely physical, that my psyche is not equally sick. Orage is convinced that Gurdjieff is a physician of the soul, and I agree with O that life can be very much more than it is. But it is not enough simply to believe this: one must know it, must live it, with mind and heart and body. I can only lie here and think and think and think—and even that exhausts me. It is all up with me; my heart and body have reached the limits of their endurance. It is common sense, to live in a three-fold way, head and heart and good sound limbs. But how much is required before we can commit ourselves to it, how much must we go through before we are convinced that it is the only way, that any other way makes us less than human...

14 October

A birthday. Well, what of that? From LM, a sprig of mimosa—and a glance of reproach.

She thinks I should continue with the treatments. But they are of no further use to me. Both Manoukhin and I know it, and I shall not see him again. Perhaps they were of some benefit to my lungs, but they did not help my heart, and that is the crux of the matter. My heart. Yesterday I thought I might die. Yes, actually— on Friday the 13th. It was not imagination. I was very frightened and, what made it worse, saw my fear mirrored in LM's face. To-day it is as much as I can do to creep from bed to desk and back again. Even a walk in the Luxembourg is out of the question to-day. Bed, chair, scribbling. The absence of all feeling, even of fear. Or if there is fear, it is fear of nothingness: not to be. But in noth-ingness there is forgetfulness, peace, and rest. This—bed, chair, pencil—is scarcely a life.

But the visitors cheered me. How good to see Orage again and to know we are here on the same errand. He has given up the editorship of New Age to come and work with Gurdjieff. His friend Dr. James Young has already been to Fontainebleau. He spoke with much excitement about Gurdjieff, the Institute, and the dances. And yet there was nothing of unthinking devotion to the Master about him. If anything, there was a touch of self-mockery. At any rate, he seemed to insist upon his right to make a critical appraisal of the place, though his overall impression was favorable. I shall wait to see for myself. It is reassuring to know that people like Orage and Young are drawn to Gurdjieff. But a decision, when it is taken, must be one's own.

Dr. Young examined me. I will do well enough, he says—for now, being his unspoken implication. Then Orage got up to go and stooped by my chair to say goodbye.

"Gurdjieff will be in Paris tomorrow. Young has arranged for you to meet with him. I will come for you around noon. It isn't far."

The news set my heart beating at an alarming pace. I could only stare at him wide-eyed. He withdrew before I could protest.

15 October, 4 AM

I have been thinking and thinking. Perhaps if I write I will come to something.

My position is hopeless. I am as ill as I have ever been, nay, worse. And there is no escape. The treatments have failed me, and every day I am a little weaker. What do I have to look forward to? The prospect that soon I will be unable to leave this room! As it stands, I can do nothing and go nowhere without LM's assistance; soon I will be a complete dependent. Yes, your position is hopeless. How to reconcile this with the organic need to hope?

I cannot work, and it no longer suffices to pretend. It exhausts me even to think of working, and what sort of work could the likes of me produce? What sort of work can come from a weakling who can scarcely lift the pen? The strange thing is that I no longer seem to want to. A voice within me says, It would not be right. Why would it not be right? It is as though some powerful force had laid its weight upon my arm, saying, Enough, no more. That part of my life is past. Then the emptiness, the fear. What is there to replace it? For there must be something. One cannot live an entirely superfluous life. It is contrary to reason. I do not believe there are any superfluous human beings—just confused people who do not know what is required of them. What then is required of you, Katherine? What do you want?

Let us take the last question first. I want that my life should be more than it seems to be, more than it is, than it has been. None of the people I know will confirm my suspicion that it can be more, save for Orage—and Gurdjieff. But what do I mean by more? What is lacking in the life I have led? What is the "something missing" without which none of the good things make sense? Speak without thinking, Katherine, speak from the heart. It is simply that there is nothing to unify this life, nothing to pull it together, nothing outside or above it to give it meaning. Or, as Chekhov has it: "When a man lacks the things that are higher and stronger than all external influences, a bad cold in the head is enough to upset his equilibrium and make him perceive an owl in every bird and hear a dog's howl in every sound." Such a person will be at the mercy of boils on the neck and indigestion and every change in temperature or altitude that does not agree with him. Not to mention a fearful and uncontrollable contraction of the heart. What does he mean, old Chekhov? What did his brother's death teach him? To write at thirty like an old man, to have a premonition of his own death, to feel the inadequacy of the resources with which he would be obliged to face it. Was he urging upon us a religion that he regarded with aversion and covert desire, that he longed for but could not espouse? Not he. As always with Chekhov, he confines himself to telling us what experience consists of, and then he withdraws, leaving us alone and wakeful.

What does your experience consist of, Katherine? Why, it is the experience of a typically false life that, in spite of its headlong course and apparent independence, is preoccupied with the opinions and the good will of others, to such an extent that I no longer seem to myself to have any opinion or will of my own that is not merely a reaction. What do I even know of the opinions of others? What do I know of what others are like? It is all inference and conjecture, and yet upon this fantasy I have founded my life. Take my lunch with Lewis at the Schiff's. It was odious, by which I mean that he behaved as insultingly as possible toward me and I was consumed with the most hateful feelings. A hateful Katherine was called forth in me and mesmerized by the animus he seemed to bear me, returning hate for hate. And what is it all for? I do not wish to hate him, I do not even wish to know him, but I am the victim of my own reactions, of all these petty 'I's, as Orage calls them, that live in me and seek to make me do their bidding. This is the way things are, and yet it is a state that cannot be allowed to continue—if I am to have any *life*.

What I want is a life in which I occupy the center, not as the object of celebrity and literary acclaim, but as the master, of my own thoughts and feelings and sensations. If that is what Gurdjieff helps people to do, then I am for him. I want the things of the world, of course, the house and child that Jack and I have dreamed of, a garden, animals, the whole beautiful world of natural things. I want to be in contact with that world, through a love and a perception that unites thought, feeling, and sensation. Trees, flowers, the earth, the sea. I want to surround myself with these. I want to feel myself—there's only one phrase that will do—a child of the sun.

And I want to be writing. How good it is to write! How it eases the heart! But the writing that I do in the future will have to come from all of me, not from one of those small fearful petty little selves who want to take revenge or parade their cleverness before the world.

What is required of me then? To thine own self be true. But which self? Is there a self that can contain the truth, that can stand it? To feel that there ought to be, to trust in people who believe in such a self, to search for it with all one's strength and being!

What is it that stands in my way? Fear. Fear of what? Of the opinion of that world I am leaving. Of losing J. But I must face it: What do I have to lose that I have not already lost? The pitying glances of friends who see what they believe to be hidden from me. They are sealed within the hermetic vessels of their own lives, their concern for husbands, lovers, children, work, and can no more know or touch mine than I can know what their experience is—or what they think of me. They do not themselves know what they think of me, and yet I allow myself to be ruled by my own imaginings. How is it that I haven't known this before now? J too, bound up in the life of his own imagining. When we are together, these separate inner lives become mixed together so that we cannot tell them apart. What I want for myself becomes what J wants for me—or what I think he wants. That is why I have separated from him: to grow calm, to come to myself. To come into possession of an inner voice I have never had. That is surely the pearl beyond price. To have that is to be beyond the petty and baleful influences that act upon Chekhov's poor Nikolai. That there should be something in me that has authority and can exercise it. That is worth a venture and a risk. That is what I must try for.

Thank God for writing. Hope is restored. Dearest, I am going today to meet with Gurdjieff in the hope that he will allow me to come to Fontainebleau. Do not think that this can come between us. Do not think that you can ever lose your place in my heart. The old feelings, the pure ones, are still untouched, still well up at the thought of you, at the whisper of your name. Nothing can change this. I would have you know it. All is well.

Evening

Orage at 11 with the news that Mr. Gurdjieff was at the Café de la Paix and could I come directly. But I was not to hurry; he would be there for a number of hours. Orage seemed flustered, and I was confused. It was all I could do to dress with care. LM had misplaced my cane, and I was impatient with her—at such a moment!

It was raining, and the tables outside the café were deserted. Orage ushered me inside. It was chilly and dark, but I noticed Gurdjieff immediately. He sat at a small table with a demi-tasse in front of him. My heart was pounding as I approached, but I forced myself to breathe as deeply and evenly as I could. Gurdjieff did not give any sign when Orage helped me to my chair; he continued to listen intently to something that his companion was saying to him. Orage introduced me to Frank Pinder, who was there to translate for me, but I hardly heard him. The he went and stood by Gurdjieff's chair and began to speak quietly with him. Pinder smiled politely and leaned back in his chair, but did not speak to me. Thus I had the opportunity to observe Gurdjieff. He was wearing a creased suit jacket that did not match his striped trousers, a white shirt and tightly knotted tie, and leather boots, laced to the ankles and caked with mud. His head was shaven and produced a striking impression of great intellectual power. Its nakedness—and the ear that protruded from it—seemed oddly enough to emphasize the fact that he was a human being, a member of the species. But it was the power emanating from his body in repose that most impressed me. He sat with his legs crossed, hands upon his knee, a cigarette held loosely between his fingers; one elbow rested easily on the arm of his chair as he leaned slightly toward Orage. But there was power in this posture. He gave the impression of a powerful animal at rest. It wasn't until later, when he stood up to leave, that I realized the source of this impression: Gurdjieff inhabits every inch of his body, and when he moves he conveys a feeling of complete assurance and control. I had a very strange thought: compared to Gurdjieff, the other people in the café, including Pinder and Orage—and myself—seemed hardly to be alive.

He seemed to be having trouble understanding what Orage was saying to him, and Orage himself was ill at ease, shuffling his feet and swaying from side to side. Gurdjieff said something to Pinder that elicited a chuckle, and Orage turned and left the café as though he had been dismissed. I felt a little tremor of panic. I was alone with the Master.

He turned and looked into my eyes, and I felt that I had his undivided attention. I had heard that Gurdjieff had practiced as a hypnotist, that he mesmerized people. Indeed that had been one of my reservations about coming here: what if in a physically weakened state I were to allow myself to fall under some kind of uncanny influence? Until we declared a moratorium on the subject, Jack repeatedly questioned me about whether I had been influenced by the ideas of Gurdjieff's system, as though he could not himself understand what it is to feel a sympathetic attraction. But of course the ideas were one thing, and the man himself quite another. At any rate I was relieved to find that there was nothing mesmerizing about Gurdjieff's glance, no trace of fixity, no quality of staring. In fact, it seemed to lack any kind of personal quality at all. It was a very composed look, to be sure, but it did not seem to make any assumptions about my being or to require anything of me. One might think that it would have been appropriate for us to greet each other, to engage in some kind of preliminary small-talk. That did not take place, and yet I felt perfectly at ease. We simply regarded each other for a number of moments, and then he spoke, I believe, in Russian.

"Why do you come to see him?" Pinder said.

This was the very question I had expected to be asked, and I launched into an elaborate explanation, dodging hither and thither, trying to talk about many different things at once, my health, my writing, my desire for a new life. I was aware of beating about the bush, and yet I was unable to come to the heart of the matter, to put my finger firmly upon the essential thing, which was—what? I could not bring it out. Gurdjieff listened to my rambling and increasingly agitated discourse with great attention, sitting absolutely motionless in his chair, a plume of smoke rising from his cigarette. When at last I had talked myself out, Pinder spoke. It did not seem that he could have conveyed half of what I had said. But I did not care. Whatever the reason for my coming there, I wished very much to be allowed to go to Fontainebleau. That was the question that most concerned me, I told Pinder.

"He says that if you want to live longer, you must go to a warm, dry climate."

"How much longer would I live?" I asked Pinder.

"He does not know."

There it was: there was no escape from it anywhere. But surely I had not hoped...

"No!" I said, speaking directly to Gurdjieff, since I felt sure that he understood. "I will come and spend the time that remains to me at the Prieuré—if you will let me."

Gurdjieff was silent for a moment. Then he tossed the spent cigarette away from him and gestured to Pinder, who got up and moved to another table where he put his head together with two other men who must have also been of the party. Gurdjieff turned back to me.

"Tell about parents."

Tears came immediately to my eyes. I felt as if a chasm had opened up at my feet. What was happening to me? I glanced at Gurdjieff. He was still regarding me with his calm, dispassionate eyes.

"My mother is dead," I said. "My father still lives in Wellington. He is a banker and a government official."

Gurdjieff nodded his head slightly—and continued to wait. The chasm was within me, an empty space in the middle of my chest, where my heart ought to be. Suddenly I felt that it was in fact dangerous for me to be here. I had a sudden revulsion from Gurdjieff and his peremptory manner. What right did he have to order people about? What right did he have to ask such questions? And yet I could not doubt that his asking was an expression of interest—a *sincere* interest such as one rarely encounters in life. Since he was interested, it seemed imperative to respond.

"My mother—was the most precious, lovely little being! She was ever so far away in New Zealand, of course, for most of my adult life, but she would write me such long, long letters about the garden and the house and her conversations with Father and how she loved social occasions of all sorts, garden parties and dinner dances and having people for high tea in the afternoons. I believe that she *lived* every moment of her life more fully and completely than—anyone I have ever known! She had an irrepressible gaiety, which I know now to have been high courage—courage to meet the difficulties life sends. Her last letters gave no hint of the suffering she had to endure."

I had looked away from him while I was speaking, and I now raised my eyes to meet his. It was the same dispassionate look, and yet I imagined that I saw a glimmer of sadness. And as I looked at him, time seemed to be arrested, and I heard the dying echoes of my own voice, its defensive note, repeating the platitudes with which I had consoled myself. It was one of my social voices, the "bearing-up-well-thank-you" voice, the voice that was engaged in carefully fashioning the image of myself that I wanted the world to see: a daughter bereaved, but consoled by so many exquisite memories. A flood of shame swept over me. I had thought to have left that false world behind. I was devastated to have taken this tone with Gurdjieff of all people, when my intention was to convince him of my need.

Without taking his eyes from my face, he unfolded his hands and placed them one upon each knee, palms downward. In that instant I remembered standing on the platform at Paddington, the new Mrs. Bowden, awaiting my mother's train, in the rear of a crowd of relations who were not in the know and thought that my mother was coming to visit *them*. In fact, she was coming to rescue me. In New Zealand I had made my presence virtually insupportable to my entire family until Father agreed to send me back to London. But within a year, behold what a mess I had made of my freedom. I was married to a man I did not love and could not live with. I was carrying another man's child. If ever an erring human creature needed rescue, I was that creature. While I felt oppressed by the awareness of having behaved very badly, I was trembling in the hope of something like—forgiveness.

With a precision that is almost photographic I see my mother step down from the train. Immaculately coifed, in a neat and stylish traveling costume, she treads her way through arms and embraces—until she comes to me, the object of her voyage. I am wearing a wide black hat trimmed with gold daisies, the sort of hat that requires an effort just to avoid brushing against doorways and furniture, my wedding hat, in fact, that Ida so disapproved of. No doubt it is an atrocious hat, but it affords me a measure of protection. I raise my eyes to my mother's face. Her skin is as flawless as a twenty year-old's, she has authority and poise and assurance—everything, in fact, that I so manifestly lack. I am ready to prostrate myself before her, to throw myself upon her mercy, to pour out the whole sordid story, all the confusion of my troubled heart and mind. I long to tell all, and to my mother, whose heart alone is large enough to contain it. But her eyes do not meet mine; they fly from my face to my hat. *You look like an old woman on her way to a funeral in Maida Vale, child. Such a hat! I want you to give it away at the first opportunity.*

All of this was before me in that impossibly elongated moment, as Mr. Gurdjieff sat patiently by, as though waiting for its effects to work upon me. I wondered if my mother had ever looked at me—if anyone had ever looked at me—with the attention and detachment of this strange man. I have said it was a dispassionate look, but that is not entirely true. There was no compassion in the sense that people usually understand and wish for compassion, no friendliness of which the condition is a premature intimacy, no well-meaning solicitude. I simply knew that I was seen and accepted—completely. And this knowledge was overwhelming. I was now aware, lurking beneath the surface of my silly description of my mother, of a grief and a longing that were so much greater than the pain of loss. For a moment I faced them, feeling the knowledge penetrate me—and then I looked away. I could stand it no longer. I knew why people fled from Gurdjieff.

"I am also very attached to my father," I heard myself say.
It was the most pathetic attempt to defend myself, and of course it did not fool Gurdjieff for an instant. He gave a slight shrug and leaned forward over his knees, as though to rise. Then, just as I breathed a sigh of relief, just as I began to think myself safe from those eyes, he shot me a sidelong glance.

"Must love parents," he said. "But with objective love. Subjective love, pretend love, is useless. First must see what is in self. Then maybe is possible."

He stood up. I made to rise too, but he motioned me to remain seated.

"Enough for this morning," he said, with a hint of a smile about the corners of his mouth. "Now rest."

He walked away, and his companions followed him to the door. I sat there with my thoughts until Orage came to fetch me. I cannot say whether it was minutes or hours later.

16 October

Young telephoned to say all is in readiness for me at the Prieuré. I am invited to visit, to come and see what we're up to, as he puts it, so very cheerfully and casually, as though the whole thing were no more than a sort of lark. Since it may be necessary for me to rest, he has secured me a room (after much "wrangling" with the "inmates"), and I am welcome to spend the night. Truly? "Upon my word of honor," he assures me. "There is no limit to what the perfect English gentleman can achieve—even in a madhouse such as this. But I don't mean to frighten you." On the contrary, his levity is refreshing. It makes me forget myself a while and the deadly seriousness of my errand.

See you tomorrow then. Cheery-bye! Oh, to be able to afford such levity!

17 October

In spite of the journey, it was a day of calm, the calm after the storm that led to my decision. I was so glad to leave my room at the Select. I felt that I had only barely escaped with my life—my *real* life, that is, the life I have not yet lived. LM was very tragic. One would think that I was about to enter military service—in my condition! I assured her that life could be no more strenuous for me at the Prieuré than in Paris. She was a little mollified, but only a little, to learn that Young would be there—she is inordinately impressed by the medical profession, without being in the least discriminating— and that Orage had arranged to smooth my way with Gurdjieff. She takes some consolation from thinking that I am only visiting the Fontainebleau place. But she cannot refrain from telling me that she has "a very bad feeling" about it. Do I have any idea of what I am letting myself in for? At this I felt the stirring of my own doubts and fears—and then suddenly a sense of peace. It is such a great relief to have come to a decision, for good or ill. I find myself moving about, slowly and meekly, like a little mouse, but a mouse with a purpose, with a destination, an aim. What if this little mouse should go astray? I feel sure that I have made the right choice, that something good will come of it. But I could not communicate my new confidence to Ida.

In the train: quietly excited. Paris did not tug at my heart strings as of old, and that made me a little sad. Perhaps that part of my life is over too. LM was silent, muffled up in her own feelings, and I was grateful. I asked her to change places with me, so that I could sit facing the direction of the train, with my back to Paris. It seemed appropriate. It was a gray day. Paris was gray and wan, not as I would like to remember it.

No sooner in motion than our journey was over. LM helping with my bags, shedding a none-too-surreptitious tear. Young waiting on the platform: Welcome to the menagerie! I remain outwardly composed, though inwardly a riot of confused emotion. What sort of reception awaits me? Will I be permitted to stay? Will I *want* to stay?

Young had engaged a fiacre. He sat facing Ida and I, his red cheery face wreathed in smiles, simply bursting with news, but inhibited by Ida's grief-stricken demeanor. The horse clattered past a timber yard, and the sharp sweet scent of the sawdust filled my heart with yearning—for what?

Past the bridge leading to Avon and out onto the Valvins Road. I closed my eyes to compose myself, and in order not to see LM's ravaged face. When I opened them again it was quite dark: we were within the wood of Gautier. In the presence of all those trees, my fortitude returned to me. I have always loved trees, their silent supplicatory nature, the dependence of great bulk upon a single trunk, their deep unseen extent within the ground. Truly they are living things and offer the unquestioning companionship of nature. I could have driven all day beneath their canopy, in their solemn half-light, rocking gently to the motion of the carriage. I felt at peace for the moment. If only such moments could suffice. But the horse was passing a tall forbidding wall, was slowing down and stopping by a pair of strong wrought-iron gates. My heart gave a little jump. I had hoped perhaps that it might be further off, that I might postpone the moment of truth just a little longer. But no. Le Prieuré d'Avon, M'sieu-dames.

I stepped out. The gates were closed; behind them a forest of overgrown shrubbery, with no glimpse of the building itself. There was a bell-handle and a sign: SONNEZ FORT. Young rang it with gusto. We waited in silence, our baggage beside us in the grass. The cocher threw himself back in his seat, lit a cigarette. What I would not have given for a cigarette! Young rang again. LM was icily composed. I turned away from her. I was trembling within, but determined not to let her see it. Perhaps no one would come. Perhaps I would be turned away. I was about to ask Young to ring a third time when a small boy of ten or eleven with a mop of hair hanging in his eyes emerged from the shrubbery.

Good Lord! It was *our* little boy, mine and Jack's, the very incarnation of a drawing I had made at the top of a letter from the Villa Flora, at the end of that awful Casetta winter when our separation had weighted so heavily. I was so pleased with myself to have caught the effect I was looking for, shy wonder and a delicate, exploring tread—and here it was in life!

He began to unlock the gates with a key that was almost as long as his arm. I stepped forward and smiled at him, but he was so intent upon discharging his function that he didn't notice me. The gates swung open to admit us.

"Patrick will show you into the house," Young told us. "I'll go on ahead and see about accommodations for Ms. Moore."
He strode ahead with our bags. I introduced myself and Ida to Patrick. He did not acknowledge the introductions in any way. His gray eyes flitted from me to Ida and back. He seemed remarkably poised, utterly at one with himself, looking out with composure at the incomprehensible world of adults. He was older than the child I had imagined, but that served only to make the resemblance the more convincing, as though the child of my imagination had grown since I had lived with him day and night at the Casetta—like a real child! It was in the spring that I sent my drawing to Jack. We were to be together in England within 27 inter-

minable days and nights, and I had allowed myself to hope again for the child of our love, and Jack, I suppose, had not the heart to say me nay...

Suddenly, without uttering a word, Patrick started up the driveway at a great pace, virtually running away from us. Come back at once! Ida called after him, in a great wax. Mrs. Murry is obliged to walk very slowly. She was probably relieved to have an object other than myself for her anger and frustration. He came back, reluctantly, but now I saw him dart a shy glance of new interest at me. Why is that? he came out with suddenly. His accent, being rather flat, was not at all like an accent I would have given to my little boy, and yet I was instantly reconciled to it. None of your business, Ida told him sharply. Please don't run off like that again. She is of the school that believes it doesn't matter if you speak sharply to children—because they are only children. I felt protective of Patrick; I would have told Ida off if I hadn't been so tired. For a moment, as though chastened, he seemed to draw a sort of screen over his eyes. But then I saw the light of interest or mischief return—and with it the uncanny presence of the child in my drawing. He walked a pace or two ahead of us with elaborate slowness, yet as lightly as a wild animal, glancing back at intervals with an affectation of great seriousness that was quite charming. Ida brought up the rear, brooding. If I stopped to rest, Patrick stopped too, and Ida came up and stood just behind my shoulder, like the Angel of Death.

The driveway was lined with colossal rhododendrons, all tangled up with other shrubs and vines. Then the bushes gave way to two rows of trees, the driveway turned, and the house was visible. It was breathtakingly beautiful. Seen across an expanse of unkempt lawn, its windows and roof a little the worse for wear, it still had a dignity, a formal symmetry that brought me up short: a chateau with three stories, the dormers of the third emerging from a steep roof, very broad in front with marvelously tall windows and solidly built wings. It had been a Carmelite convent and before that the residence of Madame de Maintenon. God only knows how Gurdjieff had acquired it. Something about the atmosphere of the ruined park drew me, the flower beds clogged with leaves, the wild shrubbery. And it seemed to be completely deserted, save for a group of chickens scrabbling about beneath the distant trees.

"Oh no! The chickens are in the flowers! Ms. Matters will have me life!"

With this exclamation, Patrick took off running like a cat across the empty lawn that lay between us and the chateau. I bit my lip to suppress a smile; I knew that for Ida the auguries were most unpropitious. I felt suddenly drained of strength. Deserted by our guide, we proceeded across the lawn at a snail's pace and entered the building by a side door. We passed down a narrow corridor, from which I could see people working in a makeshift kitchen, and went into a large room with the tall windows that I had seen from outside. Most of the room was empty, save for a couch and chairs near the windows and an upright piano. I eased myself into the couch, trying to conceal my exhaustion from Ida.

Patrick materialized in the doorway. I was mesmerized by the expression in his eyes. In my drawing, which I came across last month in Pond Street while sorting through my letters to Jack, my little boy is looking into the paper, peering at an unseen object of interest. I think I rendered him like this because I did not know what he looked like, and I was afraid to disappoint myself. But Patrick's eyes: surely I had seen them in a dream.

The chickens, he began—but Ida silenced him with an irate look. I asked to speak to Orage, suddenly feeling the need to see a familiar face. Patrick did not know him; he would go and inquire. I immediately regretted that I had sent him away. I longed to go on looking at him.

Ida settled herself at the opposite end of the couch.

"Katie, for the very last time, I implore you..."

"I shall scream!"

For all my exhaustion I felt a sense of accomplishment. I had arrived. I still had the lingering fear that Gurdjieff would turn me away, but I counted on Orage to intercede for me. He had assured me I would be able to stay the night at least. What more did I need to know? I felt confident that I could convince Gurdjieff of my sincerity, if only I were granted another audience. I began by trying to put together in my mind what I should have said to him in Paris, what I *would* say if he suddenly appeared in the doorway. But I could not retrieve any part of it. Panic-stricken,

I remembered that I had written down the record of my *crise* of two days ago, and I wondered if I would have time to rummage in my bags for my journal. What if LM had omitted to pack my note books—out of a spiteful carelessness? I was working myself up into a state over it. And then suddenly, miraculously, all of my agitation left me, as though the genius of the place had laid a gentle hand upon my spirit. How unkind to poor Ida. She is facing her own dark night of the soul. For if I stay—and I am determined to do so—it means a parting for which she is ill prepared. But I could not speak to her. I sat quietly, looking out the tall uncurtained windows, on to what had once been lawns and gardens. Some people passed at a distance, silently and purposefully, carrying garden tools. This further glimpse of the life of the place reassured me. But it seemed remote from *my* life, which was ebbing there in the ethereal half-light of the afternoon, never to turn in flood. I unwound my hat and placed it on the couch beside me and closed my eyes.

19 October

I have been assigned a small bare room with only a bed and a washstand. Ida slept on a mattress on the floor and complained that the draught under the door had given her a stiff neck.

But the great news is that I am allowed to stay—for at least two weeks. This was the outcome of our lunch today with Mr. Gurdjieff. Ida and Orage and I were guests at his table, and the decision was communicated to me by Orage. A great deal was said at table that I did not understand. Mr. Gurdjieff eats with the students who have been with him longest; many of them followed him out of Russia after the Revolution. They seem a rather serious, not to say severe company. But the chief thing, is that I have at least two weeks. To make *use* of them: that must be my aim.

In the evening, all gathered in one of the large rooms before a fire of enormous logs, virtually tree trunks. Here I witnessed some of the dances that Young had talked to me about in Paris. I cannot begin to describe them or the musical accompaniment. There is one dance called "The Initiation of a Priestess" that charged the atmosphere of the room in a remarkable way. Perhaps it would be more accurate to call it a sort of mime, since it consists of movements, postures, gestures, and intervals of dance. It communicated a feeling of joy, and at the same time, a feeling, not of sadness, but of deep seriousness. Someone told me later that it came from a cave temple in the Hindu Kush, but even without knowing this I was able to perceive its sacred nature. It produced in me a clear conviction, without a shadow of a doubt, that I have done right in coming here. If Mr. Gurdjieff is associated with such things, then I believe that he can help me. Indeed I have already been helped. Just to be here in this company, to be allowed to have contact with such things. My heart is full of gratitude.

Today Ida went to Paris in the morning to get my things from the Select. She returned in time for dinner, but instead of joining the assembly she went upstairs and spent the evening alone in our room. When I came up, transported by the dances, she pretended to be asleep. I spoke to her, and we talked for a while, and she seemed comforted. Poor Ida, she is like a fish out of water here. A week ago I should have held myself responsible and reproached myself for lack of consideration. But now I have no such feeling; I must attend to my own needs while time remains to me. This is a new experience for me, the sense of urgency and conviction in regard to what one wants. I believe I like it.

20 October

Parted with LM who had spent the night at Fontainebleau. She was distraught; it was necessary to be firm with her. But it was not a bad parting, where people go away with something horrible between them like a dead creature that has not been buried. For some reason I remembered that at the very worst of times, at the Casetta, for example, when Jack returned to London and I felt so ill and wretched and abandoned, such an invalid, at such times Ida and I have been able—after the most appalling scenes—to renew our friendship, and everything between us has been as of old. I have not treated Ida as she deserves, and the memory of it still reproaches me. I am determined to be just to her now and in the future, to be no more the old unruly Katie. But until I am well, truly well, I cannot have proper relations with anyone.

I have a new room that is nothing short of palatial. I didn't realize this last night. When Young showed me upstairs, I sat on the bed exhausted, unable even to perceive my surroundings. Young is kindness itself. Since it was obvious that I did not wish to go downstairs again, he very kindly brought me some food from the kitchen. After I had eaten, I simply tumbled into bed in my clothes. He had made me a fire. I thought that I would watch the flames and think of you, darling. But sleep simply engulfed me.

I woke early, as soon as it was light, and I am sitting up in bed, admiring my quarters. Soon I will have to go downstairs, and I must confess I am a little apprehensive about it all, but for the moment I have a little time. I am in a part of the chateau that people call "The Ritz": beautiful old wainscoting, paneled door and shutters, high vaulted ceiling, antique chairs that one is afraid to sit on, mirrors and engravings on the walls. The window frames a piece of the pale sky—"that little patch of blue that prisoners call the sky." I am a prisoner too, imprisoned in this body that will not let me live.

I have walked to the window and back. I am a little breathless. The gardens must once have looked like Versailles. I would give anything to be able to explore them, alone and unassisted. I have much to be grateful for—not least that I am here, in this place, where I have dreamed of being, that people here have been so kind. But oh! I am melancholy today. Has it something to do with the autumn, do you think? The waste of leaves strewn about the park, wispy tree tops against the pale pale sky. Oh more than melancholy—fearful! What if I should die alone, with no one beside me? There: I have said it.

That is the thing that plagues me and will not let me be. I have spent such a great deal of time alone in the past five years that I do not think I can bear any more. That is why I wrote to Jack from the Casetta to ask, to beg, Would you mind very much if I adopted a child? I wanted a baby boy if I could get one. I was convinced that I could manage as regards money. But I could not bear the suffering of being ill and alone. That's where the child was to come in. We were to take care of each other. I'd love him and he'd love me. But I could not proceed if Jack disliked the idea. For the child would always be with us, you see, when we were together, just like he was our own darling little boy. I was afraid Jack might hate that. Try to see it from my position, I implored him. A child will keep me from utter loneliness and despair, from writing desperate letters, from worrying you and keeping you from your work. If you like, I will ask Brett to be his guardian, in case anything should happen to me. For of course you could hardly be expected to take care of him if I wasn't there. Think it over, I said, and write me as soon as you can...

The letter was written in one of my horrid fevers that make everything more vivid, as a nightmare is vivid. But I could not wait for his reply. I wrote again that same day, a desperately calm and casual letter, in which I enclosed a poem entitled "The New Husband."—*Who's the husband—who's the stone/Could leave a child like you alone?*—that sent Jack scurrying to the telegram office. He was coming to see me as soon as he could arrange to leave the *Athenaeum* for a fortnight. My proposal to adopt a child was never mentioned again.

Last year: the drama reenacted with minor variations. Before Jack came to Paris from Montana, he had written to say if I *wanted* him to come, if he could be *of some use to me*, then he would come at once. Otherwise not. I urged him not to come. Before I left, it was all his work with him, the time is passing, I do not want to interrupt my novel. I felt that I was obliged to grant him his independence, as he had granted me mine in the past. His offer was not sincere. I did not feel *understood* by him. I did not feel that he had entered into my predicament. If the sun shone, he would work; if it snowed—why he might as well play cribbage with me in a hotel room in Paris! He came anyway, in spite of me, and things were as before. Back and forth to M, living at opposite ends of a long passageway, chess instead of cribbage. Writing "The Fly"—and then the forte reaction: utter prostration. Reading Wallace's book and having literally to conceal it every time Jack walked into the room. Our conversations upon the subject came always to the same impasse: Jack's absolute rejection of "occultism," tempered by his reluctance to deprive me of hope; my insistence that there was no question of "influence," that the ideas were simply my own deepest convictions writ large. It was Jack's unstated conviction that I ought to have stayed in Montana, that I had endangered to no avail the little lease of life the mountains had given me by traveling to Paris for a treatment dubious at best. He could not understand my longing for a miracle, the strength of my desire to be well. That too lay between us. And the miracle did not occur.

All that is over, all that false hope, all half-measures that address the body only. I am not well enough to look after a child. I see and accept that now. And I must live apart from Jack and seek what I know to be health for me. Impossible to live at odds with each other, feeling his unspoken reservations, suspecting his every glance, willing myself to conceal my distress from him—only to have it break out over a trifle and plunge us both into gloom. Impossible to live like this. But oh! How hard that is to bear. Is there not some way to put oneself in the other's shoes, to bear one's own burden and the other's equally, to live in understanding in spite of distress. For there is no doubt that we are *for* each other, as we have never been for anyone else. What is the root of the trouble that complicates our relationship? It is not health nor lack of health, I insist, but something more fundamental. Call it the selfishness of lovers, though the dear knows that lovers can hardly be said to have a corner on the market in selfishness. It is simply that the self comes first and all others afterwards. But it is not a choice, not a question of decision, not at all. Sometimes one positively wills the primacy of the other's needs—to no avail. The most important person in one's world is always oneself; it is a matter of perception, of perspective—no, that is not what I mean. It is an organic thing, no less a part of me than my physical body, impossible to repudiate.

And yet if I understand Orage, that is just what must be repudiated if I am to have the new life I crave. Can I believe it? It is possible to wish for the well-being of the other with all your heart. I *do* believe this. But in my path stands the devil of selfishness, waiting to devour me. If there were anything substantial, tangible—corporeal!—about this devil, you might be able to wrestle him to the ground. You would triumph over him or know the reason why. But the case is otherwise. These are just words, descriptions of experience, not the thing itself. The truth is that this selfishness operates on a visceral level, below the level of awareness, and it moves faster than thought, to seal off all escape to the pure air of a better world. It is part of the body's business, perhaps all the more so with me, The body is not the source of all my ills, but it is there the demon must be met, according to Orage, and one must seek it out with unflagging attention, in order to know it through and through.

What then? What does all this mean? How can it restore me to myself?

Dearest Jack, I believe there is a way. But in order to know it, I must draw back and separate myself from you completely, the better to know us both, to disentangle our struggling selves. Only when that has been accomplished can we come together again as one.

21 October

I have had a full and exhausting day. Now I am back in bed again, although it is early, propped up against the pillows, grateful for another of Jimmy Young's fires, which warms my heart if not my extremities. I'm tired. But it is a good tiredness, I think, a healthy normal tiredness after a day of many new impressions. I must try to set them down before sleep descends...

Orage came to visit. He is different here, somehow. Perhaps it was the baggy old suit he was wearing, for digging in the garden, he says ruefully. But no, it had nothing to do with his clothes. There was a certain concentrated quality about him, as though he had collected all his energy in order to focus it on a single point. Is that a result of whatever work he has been doing here? I cannot tell. But as he sat there, leaning on the arm of his chair, the light striking the side of his rather heavy stolid face, I felt a sudden up-welling of affection for him.

"Do you know, Orage," I said impulsively, "I cannot imagine anyone I would rather be welcomed by in this place—not even the Master himself! I feel that I owe you a tremendous debt of gratitude."

"The ideas were already your own," he murmured. "You would have found your way here sooner or later."

"Better sooner," I said.

His gaze met mine and held it. What a relief it is to meet with understanding, to face what must be faced without flinching. There was no flinching on Orage's part—and no agonized attempt to console either. He simply sat with me, while it lay between us in all its fearfulness. And I was soothed by his manner, his composure, the solid mass of him in the chair, leaning slightly toward me, regarding me with an intense interest. I felt in him a real wish for my well-being, a wish independent of whatever he might want for himself.

"You've made it possible for me to come here," I said. "But I was thinking of the past, of your encouragement of my writing." He made as if to demur, but I hastened on, feeling under some very urgent compulsion to speak my mind to the full.

"I've learned a great deal from you, Orage. Are you aware of this? If I've seemed impatient of your good advice, I've learned in spite of myself—from your example, your convictions about literature, what it is and what it could be, from your commitment to what is best. I'm afraid you must have thought me a rather dull student—must think so still! What little I have accomplished, when my work is set alongside my aspirations. But you taught me to aspire. You must take responsibility for that! You taught me to write, you taught me to think, you taught me what to do—and what *not* to do. I've come to the end of my old writing life, and a new one has not yet opened out in front of me. But when it does—as it must!—I will be guided by those aspirations you have set for me. All I've written up to this, even *Bliss*, has been tainted by the sort of life I've lived, a negative life, and a lack of a purpose, even in my work. All of that life has been swept away, and I feel that almost nothing of it remains. I want to write in a different way, to produce a new kind of writing. For this I must have a new idea that is entirely mine, something that springs not from my dissatisfactions but from my sense of being alive in the world. I don't how I will come to this idea, but if I may judge from the sharpness of my need, I *will* come to it, by hook or by crook. And you will be the first one—perhaps the only one—I will run to tell. So thank you, Orage—for everything."

I leaned back upon my pillows, somewhat short of breath, but feeling a great sense of relief, as though I'd gotten something off my chest that had lain there a long time. Orage did not reply at once. But he did not withdraw into his own thoughts. He was completely present with me in the room. It was a feeling of sharing a moment with another human being. I felt safe, content, *at home.*

"You are an exceptional person, Katherine," he said. "You would have accomplished something with or without my influence. I look at things differently since I met Gurdjieff, and I don't believe it is possible for us to know what is good for others. In fact, I blush to think of the advice I dispensed so freely, both in private and in print. But I'm happy to know that some of that well-meaning advice may have helped to light your way. It was the merest accident, you know, or great good fortune.

This was said with great simplicity, and I could not doubt that he meant it. We remained for a while without speaking. I wanted to get up and dress, to meet with whatever the day had in store. But I was equally reluctant to bring our tête-à-tête to a close. It was like a happy and unsought-for encounter in a far lonely place, not the sort of thing that could ever be repeated.

"Do you remember, Katherine," he said, "how we used to feel that art was above life, was in fact its only conceivable justification? But what kind of art have we created? The good books have all but killed my enthusiasm for literature, books without a soul, polished gems that sparkle but emit no light. We need an art that is the servant of life, that does not exalt the individual, but instead shows us our place within the larger scheme of things."

"And we shall have it," I assured him lightheartedly "There will be a new literature—I will point the way to it myself! But first I must have my idea."

"There is something in the dancing that may help you," Orage said. "You do not have to participate in order to be affected."

When I did not immediately reply, he gave a little shrug.

"It's a hard thing to have to give up one's idols. It makes one feel—old."

"You have given up a great deal just to be here. Was it worth it?"

He smiled his broad disarming smile, and at once his face was open and sunny.

"Well you may ask! I sometimes feel that I have exchanged my life for a great mound of dirt—the dirt I have extracted spade-by spade-full from the infernal holes that Gurdjieff has had me dig. One would think he was planning to turn the grounds into a minefield. But we shall see, as the blind man said."

He did not seem in the least discouraged. He got to his feet and took a step toward the door.

"I'm forgetting what I came for," he said. "Mr. Gurdjieff wishes you to be out of doors as much as the weather will permit.

You are to accompany the work group in the garden, simply to observe, from a dry comfortable seat, a chair brought from the house, if necessary. One of the children is to be assigned to you, to help with your physical needs."

His face had assumed such a serious and conscientious expression that I couldn't help beaming at him.

"We shall have a little talk every now and then. I shall so look forward to it!"

"And I!" he said gaily. Then seriously again: "You will want to take your meals with everyone, as much as possible."

"Oh I'm sure I shall be able to! Last night I was just a little tired. But today I feel—a new woman!"

"And to attend the lectures and the movements classes, not to participate, of course, but to be present."

The shadow of my illness suddenly fell over me. How wonderful it would be to take part in the dances, or even to stand by while "The Initiation of a Priestess" was being performed.

An instant of his kindly glance. Then he withdrew. The tears could not be held back, and I let them flow. I have learned not to resist my grief. It only makes things worse—and it can bring on an attack of coughing. But I thought, what is the use of my being here at all if I cannot participate in the *life* of the place? I am simply imposing myself on people and making things difficult for them—and all because I want what I cannot have and will never have: a full and healthy life.

Then I lay back and closed my eyes, in spite of my resolve to get up and go downstairs. I must have slept or dozed, for I had a sort of dream. My grandmother and I on the sea between the islands in a white boat—or a boat made pale by moonlight—a tall boat studded with lights, more fit to sail among the stars than out upon the cold sea. She asks me to carry her umbrella with the swan's head for a handle...Awoke to a sense of being obliged to travel on alone, to the loneliness of a child, separated from my beloved grandmother, sent away upon a night voyage, with only a very old and rickety, albeit kindly, swan for company.

I took my grandmother's name when I began to write, instinctively, knowing that she had loved that part of me. No, she simply loved *me*, from the moment I was born. She was the one constant presence: everyone else came and went, my father to the center of Empire on business, my mother and older sisters to England in order to accompany him on the voyage back. I knew my grandmother's love as a child, the way a child knows such things—and then I must have forgotten it. But I know it again now. Perhaps the truly important things cannot ever be lost, only misplaced.

I remembered what I had said to Gurdjieff: I am very attached to my father. And I remembered my father's response to the publication of *Bliss*, a single line in a letter filled with pleasantries: We were glad to hear your news. And how is the weather with you? It was Orage I always thought of when a story or a book came out. Even in the years when we were not in touch, it was in his estimation that I measured my accomplishment, it was on his lips I heard the praise I could not give myself. If I had done well, if I had given of my best, he was happy for me: of that I could be sure. It was my fate to come from a family and a place in which my accomplishments were not valued, were not even acknowledged. And I said to myself, What do I care about it? But now I must own that I care a great deal.

I lie on my right side and put my left hand up to my forehead as though I were looking far into the distance. Since I have been really ill, I have been granted the ability to *live* in my imagination or in memory: it is my "consolation prize." The scenes I conjure up are marvelously vivid; it is not too much to say that they are almost hallucinations. Today, for instance, I am in the house on Tinakori Road, No. 75. Mother and Chummie are still alive, but they are in the garden or at the bay. The front door is open, the windows too, the sashes lifted and the lace curtains streaming in the breeze. The house is like a ship rigged for a passage, its sails filling with a favorable wind. I glide through the hall that smells of the sea, mount the stairs, approach my father's study. He turns from his desk as I enter, in his eyes an expression that was never there, Orage's kindness, his intent and interested gaze. Father, I say, this is my little book, into which I have put the best of myself. My dear child, he says—and folds me in his arms.

22 October

My companion here is to be Adèle Kafian, a Lithuanian girl of 17 or 18 who is away from home for the first time. I was immediately drawn to her. She has the most beautiful dark eyes, so very expressive and—Russian. She does not speak English, of course, so we are obliged to converse in French, a language neither of us is fluent in. But we understand each other perfectly well. She is to be my companion, meaning that she is to see to my physical needs and to initiate me into the routine of the house. I was going to say—in so far as I can participate. But Adèle speaks with such excitement of the simplest things, of the work in the garden, for example, that I already feel a part of it without having lifted a tool or turned a sod. All that will come in due course, if it is to come. She confided in me that one must do the sort of work that one does not like here and that she feels a little guilty, since being in my company will be a pleasure for her. There was something in the simple unaffected way she said this that touched me—and gave me heart. I think we are going to be friends.

My routine: I go downstairs at 7:30 AM and eat breakfast, which consists of coffee, buttered toast, gorgonzola cheese, quince jam, and eggs. There are not many people eating at this time. Adèle informs me that most of the household rises at 6:00 AM and breakfasts on coffee and dry toast. Only visitors are permitted to deviate from the routine, and this made me realize that I'm still on probation here. Since my first day, Gurdjieff has not spoken a word to me, and I have seen him only at a distance. He seems always to be terribly busy, as though personally overseeing every aspect of the work here. But Orage says that I am to meet with him again next week: "And then we will see."

After breakfast, the weather being fine, I go into the garden and attach myself to Adèle's work group, not to take part in the physical work, of course, although I long to, but merely to observe. How wonderful it would be to get one's hands dirty, to get down on one's knees and scrabble in the earth! But I must be patient. Just as I am wondering where I am to sit, Patrick appears beside me, laboriously bearing a large channel-back chair. I am delighted to see him and to discover that my original impression has lost none of its force. He is still the child of my dream come to life.

"Please put it down," I tell him. "It looks so heavy. I am sorry to put you to such trouble."

"It is no trouble," he informs me politely.

He positions it on the spot I indicate and rocks it back and forth to make sure it is stable. It is a valuable piece of furniture belonging to the house, but somewhat the worse for wear, no doubt from outdoor use.

"Perhaps we can find a chair that is easier for you to carry," I suggest.

"Mr. Gurdjieff told me to use this one. He says I am to be your chair-carrier and to follow you about with the chair."

"Why, thank you, Patrick. That's very good of you."

He frowns, as though it is inappropriate for me to thank him.

"It is my *work*," he says, "the work Mr. Gurdjieff has given me—to look after you, and the chickens, and Mr. Gurdjieff's room—and I must do that work no matter what happens."

Then he is tearing across the lawn before I can think what to say to detain him.

There is something very affecting in his "no matter what happens." He obviously thinks the world of Mr. Gurdjieff. Is it only as a child that one has that sort of faith, the faith that "moves mountains"? Is it ever possible to recover it? Except ye become as little children, ye shall not enter. Is that what is meant? I do not have such faith—and yet I have such great need of it. How else am I to continue to believe that I will one day be well, in body and in mind? Since I could not generate this faith within myself, since I could not create it "out of the void," I looked to Jack to provide it, and it was one of the things that drove us apart. For what could he do but mirror back my own fear? I see it now. Orage said to me that great need attracts that which is needed, if one only has patience. And time. I have a great need of a new faith, in myself, in my writing, in the possibility of health. But do I have time?

Adèle's group is engaged in staking out the ground for a kitchen garden and constructing a kind of raised bed which will be planted in the spring. Most of the people simply ignore my presence. They seem absorbed in their work to the exclusion of any appreciation, or even awareness, of their surroundings. This strikes me as odd—and unnecessary: if one's object in being here is to wake up, these people at least seem to be determined to sleep more soundly. But surely I wrong them. It's just that I feel excluded by them, and this feeling of exclusion, if I understand what I have heard, is just what I must observe. At any rate, I am not entirely ignored. Every now and then Adèle trips to my side and gives me a bright quizzical look, as if to say, "All right?" I smile and nod my head. And when there is a pause in the work—after one of the stops, for example, when the entire group stands motionless and in silence for at least a full minute—Jimmy Young will materialize next to me and entertain me with ironical comments upon the task in hand. Most of the people have never lifted a spade in their lives, he assures me, they are taking great pains, to be sure, but they are making a most unholy botch of the job. Somehow I feel that the success of the kitchen garden is only one of their aims, and a secondary one at that.

When it came time to down tools, I saw Patrick making a beeline for my chair across the lawn. My spirits rose at the sight of him. He arrived beside me, flushed and serious. Mr. Gurdjieff had instructed him to ask if there is anything I require.

"Tell Mr. Gurdjieff I am being very well looked after and please thank him for his concern."

He frowned and looked as though he might rush off again. I was desperate to keep him.

"Did Ms. Mathers really get upset on account of the chickens?" I asked.

"Pardon?"

"On the day I came. You opened the gate for us. You said that Ms. Mathers would have your life because the chickens were in the flowers."

A scowl passed over his face. I was afraid I had said the wrong thing.

"Miss Madison," he said distinctly. "Matters is what we call her. I mean," he added officiously, "what the children call her, because she has so many *matters* to attend to. She is *always* upset."

Miss Madison, I knew from Adèle, was one of the English students, a middle-aged, unmarried woman, unaccompanied by friends or companions, whom Mr. Gurdjieff had chosen to oversee the running of the Institute on days when he was obliged to be in Paris.

"She said she would kill Jeremiah," Patrick said, pouting ferociously.

"Goodness! Who is Jeremiah?"

"One of my chickens."

"You have given them names?"

"Of course," he said, a little defensively. "The better to call them, to tell them where to go and what to do. Before they had names, they never listened to a word I said."

"And now they listen?"

"They know their names."

"And what are their names?"

"Harold for King Harold, Ptolemy for Ptolemy's Theorem, Jeremiah and Job from the Bible, and Obstinate, Pliable, Talkative, and Mr. Worldly Wiseman."

Had he read his Old Testament then, and *The Pilgrim's Progress*? No, but his English grandfather had read them and told him all the stories. Did I like the names?

"Very much," I said. "They are excellent names. But why did Miss Madison threaten Jeremiah?"

"Because he got in among her flowers. She said she will kill the next chicken she finds in her garden. She said it was my fault there was a hole in the fence around the chicken pen. But now I've fixed it. Miss Madison doesn't care for chickens, for people either. She only likes flowers. If you are ready to go in, I'll take your chair."

As I walked back to the house with Adèle, I noticed her looking at my rings, the one Frieda gave me when she and Lawrence were married, her former wedding ring that I have worn ever since, and the cluster of rubies chosen for me by Jack when I was at last free to marry him.

"Votre mari?" she asked shyly.

I explained as best I could. Jack had responsibilities that kept him in London. You have children? she said, misunderstanding. No, but we would like to, as soon as I am well. She smiled, as though relieved. But he will come to see you soon? she wanted to know. I explained to her that he was not interested in the ideas. She pondered. Perhaps if he were to visit the Institute...

"He *will* come," I assured her. "But not until I am ready to receive him. I am not fit company for anyone in my present state." She looked sad. She is just a girl, I said to myself, and you will give her a queer impression of love and married life. Besides, there is so much more to Jack and I than this separation, isn't there? Still and in spite of all?

"I will write and tell him about all the good people I have met here," I said.

"He writes?"

"Every day! We have been separated before. We are used to it. And sometimes, after a separation, there is the most perfect harmony between us. In spite of our differences, we are really like two sides of the same coin, separate and distinct, yet making one completed whole. The separations are painful, but the reunions— oh, what joy! I see myself reflected in him, not as I appear to others, or even to myself, but as I really am. And I believe it is the same with him. So that to be together is above all else an act of faith in ourselves."

She could not have understood me. But she was gazing at me eagerly, with shining eyes.

"And to be apart from each other," I said, "is like being separated from myself."

I felt the tears start to my eyes. If I continued on like this, I would lose the ground I had struggled so hard to hold. It was true that without Jack I felt estranged from myself. But that is an old self, a selfish and insecure Katherine, a self that has to die. Don't feed it! With all my heart I wish for the birth of a new Katherine, who can meet with Jack on an equal footing, who will bring out the best self in him.

Adèle had noticed my tears. Lightly, with the delicacy of a bird, she touched the other ring.

"And this one?"

"A present from my husband," I managed to say. "To mark our engagement."

My heart was torn between the resurgence of my feeling for Jack—and the reality of his absence. Adèle smiled wistfully and withdrew her hand.

"How beautiful," she murmured. "How well it suits you, the dark red color.

At noon—dinner, a very large meal with odd dishes like beans mixed with raw onions, vermicelli with icing sugar and butter, veal wrapped in lettuce leaves and cooked in cream. One is very well looked after here: it's Gurdjieff who creates the menu.

There is only one thing that I wish—to be allowed to eat in the main dining room, the Russian dining room, with all of the students. I want so much to be part of the life here, to be involved to the fullest possible extent of my powers. But I have been assigned to a smaller dining room, where I eat with the English residents and with the various guests and probationers like myself, in short, with those who for whatever reason, disability or disinclination, do not take a full and active part in the work of the Institute. That I should be obliged to share a table with tourists and curiosity-seekers, with those for whom the Institute is merely a diverting spectacle, at the very moment when I am longing to throw myself body and soul into its work—this is very hard. But I must bear it as well as I can. It is a lesson for the false Katherine, the one who cannot abide people if they are the "wrong" people, who speaks honey and thinks poison...

"Are Patrick's parents here at the Institute?" I asked Adèle as we sat alone with our coffee at the end of the meal.

Her face assumed the expression of one who is about to commit an indiscretion.

"His parents are estranged," she murmured. "His father lives in America, and his mother is in England. She is not in good health. Patrick is the ward of his aunt and her companion. They are Americans, writers, I think. I have never spoken to them."

I felt a little involuntary twinge of resentment and found myself glancing about the room.

"Are they here? Would you point them out to me?"

"They are not here now. They live in Paris."

"But what about Patrick?" I said, trying to conceal my indignation.

"They have left him here so that Mr. Gurdjieff can take charge of his education."

"But what sort of an education can he receive here? This is not a school."

Adèle gave me a mute reproachful glance. I regretted my unwarranted passion.

"I'm sorry," I said. "It's just that he's such a delightful child."

"He has a special relationship with Mr. Gurdjieff," Adèle said. "But it's not the same as having a mother and father," she added wistfully.

After dinner the garden again, weather permitting. At 4 o'clock there is tea, and after tea, any old job that is going until dark, when all knock off work and prepare for supper, a mercifully light and simple repast, at 7. After supper a crowd gathers around an enormous fire in the salon, and there is a talk by one of the senior pupils or music and dancing. Orage is right: the dances—or movements, as they are sometimes called—have opened before me the possibility of a different kind of art. It is an art that speaks not just to the mind, but to body and mind and heart together. Perhaps that goes without saying: it is the principle underlying everything that we do here. The art of the movements takes a longer view, it is a familiar of the ages, it comes to us from the depths of time and attempts to show us our place, not the place occupied by the individual, who is reduced to nothingness in the face of the cosmic pageant, but our place as a species, a living organism in the midst of titanic events—

How unlike the art I have known, the art of my contemporaries, small minds in cramped places, having nothing to offer but the concerns of a small and petty self! This is what Jack has failed to understand, though he has chastised this small-minded art. The art he would put in its place has intellectual integrity only and knows nothing of heart and body. Jack is aware of this, in the best of his poetry, but he cannot bring himself to embrace it. Perhaps if he were here, if he could see the dances. Here is the art of which I have dreamed. As yet I cannot make it my own. But I am confident that when I write again—when I am ready to express a sense of the purpose and meaning of my existence—my idea will come to me, the idea that will enable me to write in a new way. That time is still far off. For now, my job is simply to watch and wait, to stay awake—unlike Christ's sleepy apostles!—and to absorb and digest impressions.

23 October

Tonight I had an encounter. Normally Jimmy Young comes and makes me a good fire. Then I sit up watching it; I cannot sleep until early morning, if at all. But tonight he did not come and I was forced to go out of my room and wander up and down the corridors in search of firewood. All the boxes were empty. I found a stone staircase at the end of a long passage and began to descend. Footsteps ascending. Around the corner came one of the most graceful of the dancers, a young Russian woman whose name I do not know, carrying an armful of logs. We enacted a little pantomime on the stairs in the dramatic light of a naked bulb high on the curved stone wall. I was cold (shivering, clutching my shoulders, rocking back and forth), I was going downstairs (that much was obvious), in search of the very commodity she had in her arms (patting a log affectionately). Did she know where such fine logs were to be found? (frowning and scratching one's head.) Her glance was so lovely—laughing and gentle, absolutely unlike people I have known. A smile of comprehension, a toss of her head. She gave me a log, and we went our ways...

Now I am sitting up with this log, watching it burn. This is the hardest part of my day. My energies are spent, and I have no strength to keep unwelcome thoughts at bay. It is hard to be wakeful while the house sleeps, to have nothing to do save to fight a running battle with one's fears. Sometimes my longing for Jack is so strong as to threaten my very life. I feel that my body cannot sustain such a longing for another moment. I have no doubt of my decision to come here: I am spared that. But I wonder if I will be able to benefit from the place as a healthy person could. If I will have the time. And yet I have time and enough tonight, more time than I could possibly want, it passes with excruciating slowness, it falls in slow motion from the vault of night, it crawls down the old walls, it wallows upon the floor, and the only sound is one's own breathing, the only sensation the little hectic beating of one's heart, like the beating of a bird's wings against its cage...

Enough, Katherine! Enough self-pity. I will take refuge in things, the firelight on the walls, the red crumbling shell of the log, the glance of the Russian woman on the stairs. Sleep will come when it will come.

24 October

I have made another friend here. Last night, just as I rose from bed and seated myself by the fire, wrapped in blankets like a mummy, having given up all hope of sleep—came a knock to the door. It was the woman I had met on the stairs—with an armful of wood for my fire!

"I was afraid that one log would not keep you warm," she announced.

"You speak such perfect English!" I exclaimed, astonished. "Where on earth did you learn?"

"I had a governess when I was a little girl, in Russian and in Turkey. I am Montenegrin. Later I studied by myself, as part of my work in the Institute. When we met on the stairs, I could not speak to you, although I knew that you were English. I was trying to retain the energy I had accumulated during the dancing."

"How interesting. You must tell me how to do that some-time—if it is possible. I need someone to explain to me what is going on here, on the inside, I mean. And I feel that I understand you better than most of the English people here."

"Thank you," she said shyly. "My name is Olgivanna."

"And I am Katherine. Please—won't you sit down?"

I was seized by the fear that she would vanish as quickly as she had come and leave me to my awful night-time thoughts. But she bent down to the fire, placed a log among the embers, and drew up a chair. We sat for a moment in a comfortable silence. Her girlish features and a great mass of hair drawn into a bun at the nape of her neck made her look a little like Virginia, and in-deed sitting with her in silence I felt something of the ease and repose that I have only had with Virginia, after one of our discus-sions of writing, when our understanding of each other seemed so perfect and complete.

"What do you do in life?" she wanted to know.

Her question, though kindly meant, dispelled my repose.

"I am a writer," I said simply.

But of course it is anything but simple: a writer who does not write, who cannot write until a revolution has taken place within her.

"Do you write plays?" she said eagerly.

"I'm afraid not."

"Do you write novels?"

"No," I said with a pang of regret. "No novels either. Only stories—and short stories at that."

"I would like to read them."

"I will give them to you. But they're not much. I haven't written what I would like to write."

"Some day you will."

The simple conviction with which she said this lifted my spirits.

"Tell me about yourself," I said. "How long have you been at the Institute?"

"About four years. First at Tiflis. Then at Constantinople. Then Berlin, Dresden, Paris. Now here in Fontainebleau."

Four years! Four years of work, four years of devotion to the ideas, four years of association with Gurdjieff. Oh, to have four years!

"I wish I could have been with you," I told her. "Did you come to learn a great deal about yourself? Did you work as hard all the time as people do here?"

She tossed her head and gave a girlish laugh.

"Oh, I never work hard enough! I am very lazy. I could work much harder—but I don't. That is what I have learned."

I thought at once of my dreadful writing habits, of how I had wasted hours and days, simply because I would not sit down to work, because something in me would not submit to my wish to work. Olgivanna had seen the same thing in herself, but in spite of her youthfulness there was something wise and accepting in her attitude toward it. Whereas in my attitude—and I realized it for the very first time in that moment—there was only anger and intolerance toward myself.

"Only in the movements do I seem to approach my capacity for work—and even in the most sacred dances, I am so easily distracted," she said gaily. "Mr. Gurdjieff witnessed these dances in monasteries in the East and received permission to teach them. Sometimes he shows us the very ancient movements, and sometimes he makes up movements of his own. I have been in classes where we studied all day and into the night—until people dropped to the floor with exhaustion!"

Her words brought forth a great longing in me. To strive towards your goal until exhaustion overtakes you. To know what you must do and to strive with all your strength to do it, while strength remains. But I am already exhausted. And I have not yet begun to work.

Olgivanna sat looking at me, as though waiting for me to unburden myself.

"What am I to do here?" I heard myself say in an anguished rush. "How am I to work?"

She smiled slowly, knowingly.

"That is the question we must all ask ourselves. What have you seen since you have been here? In yourself, on the inside?"

"I am very grateful to be here. Truly. And yet it seems to me that I have been filled with objections to people and things. Take the English here, for example. I am not English, as a matter of fact. I have lived in England, but I come from New Zealand. It may seem to you that I am just like them, but I assure you I am not. There is a great difference between being born in England and growing up with all things English—and coming to England as a young girl from the farthest outpost of Empire. Embrace England as you may, you are an incurable provincial and must always be made to feel it. Or so at least *I* feel—and that is what matters. I so resent the English for their attitude of innate superiority. I never wanted to become so English that I forgot my own country; I long for New Zealand with all my heart. But England was my choice—and France my refuge from it. Now I find so many English here that my resentment of them has flared up again. Why are they so quiet and cold and self-contained? Why can they not take a simple pleasure in the garden? I want to feel sorry for them, but I suspect that they have some secret that cannot be communicated to the likes of me, and they hug this secret to their cold hearts. Is there a secret? Or have I simply allowed my resentment to get the better of me?"

Olgivanna dropped her eyes and stared for a moment into the fire. I thought I had committed some dreadful faux pas. Then she shot me a wicked look.

"Aren't they awful?" she burst out.

And we both fell into uncontrollable giggling, like a pair of schoolgirls. It was an immense relief.

"Simply awful," I sobbed, wiping the tears from my eyes. "But I must be serious if I am not to be sent away. I must take myself in hand."

Olgivanna opened her beautiful eyes wide and stared into mine.

"In answer to your questions," she said seriously, "Yes, there is a secret—and yes, your resentment has gotten the better of you."

"That is what always happens," I said, grateful to be understood. "No matter where I go, I find that there are people I positively *hate*—and all for no good reason. I have tried to reason with myself, I have tried to be good, but it is all to no avail. I cannot seem to help myself. It is as though there were some kind of beast inside of me, an unruly animal, a dog that will not come to heel."

"You are absolutely right," Olgivanna said eagerly. "We cannot help ourselves."

"Oh dear. Then what is to be done?"

Olgivanna was silent—until I began to fear that she was not going to answer my question.

"I don't know if you have noticed yet," she began, "how Mr. Gurdjieff treads on people's corns, as he calls it. He will frequently act so as to give offense or embarrass you in front of others. Why does he do this? The Work requires us to struggle with our negative emotions, but so few of us are capable of this, and many here do not even realize the need. If I do not acknowledge to myself that I hate such-and-such a person, how can I *see*? Mr. Gurdjieff provokes you in order to show you that this negative emotion is *in* you, that it is yours, that you are responsible for it, even though, as you rightly say, you cannot control its comings and goings."

My feelings must have been clearly written on my face, for Olgivanna reached out and touched my hand lightly.

"I do not say that Mr. Gurdjieff will provoke *you*," she smiled.

"I think he already has," I said, remembering his questions about my parents.

"Then perhaps you have already seen something of what is in you. That is the work."

"To *see* it? Simply to *see* it?"

"To see it is not the same as to know that it is there. When I first came to Mr. Gurdjieff, I suspected the existence of the animal in myself, but I did not want to *see*. To see means to acknowledge. Perhaps you will understand if I say, to see something in yourself means to *be* with it, without nervousness, without turning away."

Did I understand? I understood what the words meant. But had she put it in a different way, I might have understood more readily. My habit—or rather my great pleasure—has always been to go straight at a problem, to confront it, to surround it on all sides—with words! But something in Olgivanna's precise manner of speaking, in her careful, all-but-perfect English, beautifully tinged with the faintest note of her native place, gave me pause.

"Bring all your attention to yourself and your own responses to people," she said emphatically while I pondered. "Forget about understanding the motives of others. What matters is what is evoked in you—assuming that you want to *see*."

The wicked gleam I had noticed before reappeared in her eyes.

"These English are your friends," she said with a grin. "Seek them out. Work with them."

At this, a little shiver of discouragement went through me. I felt that this work was intended for more robust natures than mine. And the beast in me, the dog ready to turn on someone, was stronger than I.

But Olgivanna had divined my thought.

"I am terribly bad myself," she said simply. "I have such awful thoughts too! But let us work at this together. Let us try to help one another."

She rose and placed another log on the fire.

"Now I must go."

She knelt in front of my chair for a moment, gazing up into my eyes. Following a sudden impulse of affection, I put out my hand and lightly touched her hair. Then she was gone, leaving me to my fire and my thoughts.

But she also left me with such an exquisite feeling of ease, of self-acceptance. It is not pleasant to see what one is like, and yet—might it not make all the difference in the world?

25 October

Insomnia. Like Chekhov's poor Nikolai, also waiting to die, it has become the central fact of my existence and threatens to swallow everything else. I lay abed yesterday morning, hoping to steal a few hours to make up for a night of wakefulness. No such luck. I drowsed in my chair in the garden, felt so exhausted that I had to forgo the dancing and came up to my room immediately after supper. But there is no reprieve. The minute I lay my head on the pillow—no, the minute I simply look at it!—I am immediately, incorrigibly wakeful. It is as though I have run through the portion of sleep allotted me by my Maker, burned it up heedlessly in the days of my youth so that now my store is hopelessly depleted. You've been a perfect profligate of sleep, my girl—no more for you now, for the rest of your days!

Not to mention my aches and pains. I'll *not* mention them. But they have taught me something these past three years. My world has been changed by suffering; it has *depth*, it is no longer surface only. No, that is not what I mean. There is still the surface world, but there are other worlds too, not in some other place or plane, but coexisting. To see this is—an immense privilege, however one cries out against it. That is fear. How to overcome it? The winds blow, the sun disappears and the sea turns the color of slate, the little boat enters the dark fearful strait, and our prayer is, Why me? Why must it happen to me? But it's useless to utter such a prayer. There is no one to reach down and pluck us from the billows. Better to sit still—and uncover one's eyes.

I lie here and relive it all, over and over, down to the smallest detail, everything, over and over...

The house at the bay, Father striding up the garden path, the toiler returned and eager for attention, calling out for *you*, Mother, and you alone: "Hullo, Darling. Did you have a good day? The children behaved? Splendid! Are we to have that duck?" And Mother: "A perfectly lovely day, dear, the most perfect. I spent it sleeping in the garden. Oh! the children! They're as strong and healthy as a flock of young geese—and just about as unruly. I haven't the faintest idea where they are. I hope they haven't drowned—or gotten tossed by a bull!"

The lamps are lit against the encroaching dark. From the bay comes a dull snoring noise, the ocean restless in its sleep. The members of the family emerge from their various sanctuaries: Granny Dyer, Belle, we children. Mother is wearing a cameo on a black velvet band about her throat—for Father. Her beautiful face is flushed and animated. There is a smile on her lips as she bustles about the table, but there is a look of strain too, as though her skin were stretched too tight. Father, very red in the face and pleased with himself, carving knife poised over the golden duck. All this I see from within and without, feeling the warmth of the family about me like a blanket, standing outside the window like a ghost, peering in...

"Run along, children," Father says. "Can't you see your mother's worn away to a thread?" Too worn even for a goodnight kiss? "Run along now, children." Father bending over her chair where she lies in an attitude of abandonment, eyes closed, head flung back, hands behind her head, the cameo on its velvet band at her throat...

I am sitting at the top of the stairs to the third floor. The house is dark and quiet. It has a special atmosphere that one never encounters by day or when there is somebody there. You are alone, it seems to say, and that will never change. No one sees you, no one can see. This is an immutable law. But tonight this fate is relieved by a faint light gliding the stairway and the murmur of voices from the kitchen. Everybody is sleeping, but Father and Mother are still up. I shiver a little in my nightgown, wrap my arms about my knees. I am keeping them company, warming myself at the reflected heat of their attraction. The incoherent sound of their voices fills me with a sweet agitation. So long as they are wakeful, I am not alone in all the still and darkened house.

A creaking on the stairs. Shadows of the banisters dancing crazily in the light of a candle. I shake off sleep and cold and peer down upon the landing below. A voice, my mother's, but not like her, distorted with—weeping? A spasm of fear in the pit of my stomach.

"But you are *killing* me, killing me, as surely as if you had thrust a knife in my heart! Three great lumps of children and another on the way. You know I am frail. The doctor has told you that my heart is affected, that I may *die*. Then why do you—?

"Hush, Darling. You're over-tired. You mustn't feel that you have to stay up for my sake."

The voices are perfectly audible now. The banisters move with the movement of the candle, as though dissolved into smoke, but there is no more sign of the figures of my parents than if they were two ghosts conversing in a ruined house. My mother's voice, sharp and ringing, sounding brass:

"You don't love me! If you did you would never—"

"Darling! I worship the ground you walk on. I would do *anything* for you."

48

My father's voice, cajoling, reasonable, as though reasoning with a child, only more patient, less peremptory. Somehow the contrast between his composure and my mother's distress makes everything even more dreadful.

"I hate it! I hate it! You are crushing the life out of me, all of you, with your ceaseless demands."

"Annie," my father says coldly. "Do you want to rouse the entire house?"

Quiet for a moment. The banisters are motionless. I am holding my breath in fright, afraid to let it out. Then conclusively and distinctly, oh so distinctly:

"You *never* loved me. I would leave you tomorrow—if I had anywhere to go!"

My father's shocked tones:

"Darling! You don't know what you're saying. You're distraught. Think of the children."

"I think of nothing else! They never leave me alone for a minute. To think of having another! I'll never survive it. And the worst of it is..."

Her voice falling to a whisper, a sob, tightening the knot in my stomach, constricting my throat, as though this grief were mine:

"The worst of all is that I have no feeling for them, by the time I am finished bearing them I have no warmth left to give them, I do not love them—"

Weeping such as I have never heard before. Strange unnamable sounds, the expression of great distress—and it is my mother who makes these sounds. Something is clamoring for expression within me too, but it beats itself uselessly against the walls of a sealed room. My mother's weeping becomes muffled, breaks out again, subsides, dies away to a whimper. My father murmurs inaudibly. He is unshaken, constant, firm: the rock against which her grief dashes itself to pieces.

I wish that I were lying far below sleep. That is all I have to do: to sleep. Already I know that what I have learned does not belong to day. When day comes I will be safe from it. But first sleep.

A renewed creaking on the stairs, the trembling of the banisters, the bowed shoulders of my parents as they come into view, huddled together, moving with tiny steps toward the bedroom door. Father continues to murmur reassuringly as he guides Mother, his arm about her waist, supporting her, bearing the candle high. The most fearful thing is her silence. Something is broken within her, irrevocably. A sudden mad impulse comes over me. I want to rush downstairs and confront them there on the candle-lit landing. It occurs to me that somehow my presence will make it all right. I will be no trouble to you, Mother, I want to say, for after all I am almost ten years old, and I am able to look after myself.

I scramble to my feet, no longer careful. The door closes behind them. The stairs and the hall are plunged in darkness.

That was a parting of sorts, but not the real sundering. For hope is a resilient thing, especially in a child; it takes more than a single blow to kill it. The real parting took place in the Hotel Kreuzer in Worishofen, to which my mother had transported me shortly after her arrival in England, in order to separate me from Ida, my alleged partner-in-crime, and to put me beyond the reach of scandalous talk and idle curiosity. Exile was not the worst of it; I wasn't sorry to get away from London, from associations that were painful. I was even able to appreciate the luxury my mother created about her as she traveled, effortlessly, as though exacting a tribute to her beauty and her aristocratic mien.

No, the worst of it, Mother, was the ruin of my hopes of being heard. You simply weren't interested in me or in my story: that is the plain unvarnished truth, isn't it? Everything in your background and character disposed you to discount the psychological element of the situation and to bring your considerable organizational skills to bear upon the external difficulties. From a minor irritant I had developed virtually overnight into Miss Serious Problem. Serious problems require serious remedies.

My mother's suite at the Hotel Kreuzer, from the luxury of which I was to be cast out the very next day. I am sitting on the window seat, and she is standing by her trunk in the middle of the room, carefully drawing on the gloves that match her hat and subtly echo one of the colors of her scarf.

"You are twenty-one years of age, Kathleen, and so I can only advise you. My advice is that you should have nothing further to do with Ida Moore. Her family has sent her and her sister for a holiday to the Canary Islands. This will give you a pretext to sever your relations with her—if pretext is needed."

She examines the gloves and flicks a spot of dust.

"As for the rest," she says, wrinkling her nose as though at an unpleasant smell, "I can only urge you to reconsider your decision to separate from Mr. Bowden. He is not the partner I would have wished for you, but you have chosen him, and I must assume that your choice was based in some feelings of affection. He is aware of your relations with Ida and has taken no steps towards divorce on these grounds. Be sensible, Kathleen. Ask yourself if you might not be reconciled with him. If nothing else, it would add a semblance of respectability to your unfortunate position!"

This last statement is uttered with a little heat and vehemence. Our eyes meet for an instant. I look down at the floor. When I look up again, her handsome face has assumed the cast of a decision.

"It would make things easier for your family," she tells me, glancing swiftly about the room as though to see if she has mislaid anything. "But of course that is the very last thing on your mind!"

A knock at the door. A porter enters with a little hand cart and begins to wrestle with her trunk. She stands by, expressionless, lips set in a firm line, until he has maneuvered it out of the door and into the corridor.

"Come and kiss your mother goodbye."

Mechanically I rise from my seat. I feel like a disembodied spirit, existing at a great remove from the material world; my body, in particular, seems like a species of afterthought that I drag about with me unwittingly, its connection with my being entirely provisional. I cannot feel it, though I still receive reports of its state. What would my mother say if she knew that I am pregnant?

She turns her head as I approach, and I press my lips to her immaculate cheek. When I draw back, I am surprised to find that she is looking at me, as though actually making an effort to divine my state.

"This has been a most unfortunate business," she says. "I am hard pressed say what possible good might come of it. I can only hope that when next we meet—"

She stares into my eyes expectantly.

"Thank you, Mother," I say. "For everything."

She tosses her head and tugs at her glove, an impatient gestures that reveals that she takes my response for defiance—whereas it is no more than wretchedness.

"See that you adhere to the regimen here. It is costing me enough—for cold baths and wholesome exercise that one could just as well prescribe for oneself!"

I have an impulse to ask what she thinks this regimen will effect, when the opposite—warm water and sunny weather—has been prescribed for Ida. But I am too numb to be moved by anger.

My mother goes briskly to the door. I can see that she is displeased with me, for what she regards as a lack of warmth in my goodbye. This is the last straw. I am close to tears.

"There is one thing you must know, Kathleen. You are a married woman now, and it is the responsibility of your husband to provide for you. You will still receive your allowance from your father as before, and you may be thankful that he continues to be so generous to you in spite of the way you have hurt and disappointed him. But I must think of my other children and the disposition of my personal estate. As soon as I reach Wellington, I will be obliged to revoke your trust and to exclude you from my bequest. I bear you no ill will, but under the circumstances..."

She goes out and closes the door firmly and deliberately. I hear her brisk footsteps recede down the corridor. I am trying to grasp the fact that this is our goodbye, that this is what it consists of. Revolt flickers for a moment: how can she do this to me? But then it subsides, quenched by the force of her conviction. I go back to the window seat, sit, and look out. But I do not see anything. I am absorbing the blow. I am corroborating her conviction. I have brought it all on myself. I do not deserve better.

It was a month later, in a pension in the town, that I lost my child.

Those letters you used to write me, Mother, that began with a detailed weather report and went on to enumerate and describe all the flowers and shrubs that happened to be blooming in the garden, those letters, broken off after the news of my marriage and your flying visit to London, resumed again without preamble, without a single reference to my fall from grace, those letters that I treasured as proofs of my reinstatement in your affection, I now find that they are not important to me, that I can derive no consolation from them at all. This is what Gurdjieff has shown me so far. It is a painful realization, but it is accompanied by a sense of relief. I no longer have to pretend, before others, before myself, that everything was fine within the family circle. It was not fine. What it was I do not know. In spite of all my protestations, I could never see it, engaged as I was in my struggle to escape from a world inimical to my aspirations, and later from the toils of justification and guilt. Now that there is no longer any way out of my predicament, now that so many doors have been closed, my wish is only to see, as clearly as possible, what my life has been, what it really is—now and in this place.

27 October

An encounter with Gurdjieff. Patrick had carried my chair into the forest, where Mr. Gurdjieff and a large contingent were engaged in what Patrick calls a "scurry" party, from Mr. Gurdjieff's shouted exhortations, "Skorey! Skorey!"—Quick! Quick! The people in the work party, mustered hurriedly from the garden and the house, were rushing about in a small clearing, slashing with knives at the undergrowth, stooping to pick up debris, digging, tugging, pushing, and pulling—pursued, or so it seemed, by the agile Mr. Gurdjieff, who seemed to be everywhere at once.

I lapsed into my chair; the spectacle had literally made me feel tired. But I was grateful to be in Gurdjieff's presence. He still had not spoken to me, and although I was literally bursting with the impressions I had received since my arrival and with vague and half-formed questions, I could think of no satisfactory way to approach him.

Patrick seemed wholly absorbed in watching Mr. Gurdjieff. He had brushed a sliver of his long limp hair out of his eyes and stood a few feet behind my chair, one hand clamped to the crown of his head, a characteristic pose, as though holding a toupée in place. His freckled face was solemn and immobile. In Gurdjieff's presence, he had ceased to pay any attention to me.

I became aware of a movement at the far side of the lawn, in the vicinity of Miss Madison's flower garden.

"Patrick," I said. "I think your chickens are on the loose again."

He gave a start and muttered something under his breath.

"Run quickly," I told him. "I'm sure they haven't done any damage yet."

"No, no. I can't leave you alone. No matter what happens."

He looked about him frantically, as though seeking a visible way out of his dilemma.

"I am perfectly all right," I laughed. "And besides, any one of these people can render me assistance, if I should need it."

"No, no," Patrick insisted, almost beside himself with suppressed impatience. "These people have to scurry."

"Then ask Mr. Gurdjieff, for goodness sake. I'm sure he won't mind. I'll ask him myself if you won't. Think of your chickens!"

No sooner were the words out of my mouth, then I saw Mr. Gurdjieff stalking toward us. My resolve vanished in an instant. He came up, glanced at us peremptorily, and turned again to survey the activities of the work party. I was quite speechless, to my great embarrassment. I felt that I was letting Patrick down.

At length Gurdjieff turned to Patrick and indicated the place beside me.

"Patreek. Fetch chair."

He turned back to his observation of the work. Patrick took off across the grass. I watched as his small intent figure dwindled. It seemed that he slowed his pace when he passed the place where the chickens were promenading, but without stopping or deviating from his course he rounded the corner of the chateau and disappeared. A few moments later he reappeared, or rather another chair, the mate of mine, came into view, propelled toward us by a pair of short but extremely active legs. The chair grew in size, the motion of the legs accelerated, until a breathless Patrick dropped it between the standing figure of Gurdjieff and me.

Gurdjieff turned and opened his eyes very wide, as though a chair was the very last thing he expected to see. Then he hissed at Patrick:

"Skorey! Save chickens!"

Patrick took off again across the lawns like a thing possessed. This time he made a beeline for the garden. I wanted to watch his progress, but I was aware of Gurdjieff's presence. He had seated himself in the other chair in a rather striking posture, both relaxed and alert, back upright, leaning slightly forward, the palm of the left hand cupping his knee with the elbow thrust forward, while the other forearm rested loosely across his right thigh. I had longed to speak with him, but now that the opportunity presented itself, I did not know what to say. I was afraid of sitting with him—and afraid lest he get up and return to the scurry party. Therefore, I blurted out my difficulty.

"Mr. Gurdjieff," I said hastily, "I feel a great wish to do this work. When I am alone, all sorts of questions run through my head. But now that I am with you, I do not know where to begin."

He looked at me for a moment without turning his head toward me, and then he was silent for a while, as though pondering my question.

"Is no matter," he said. "Wish is what matters. Wish—the most powerful thing in the world. If you wish—you can have. But you must wish with all your being, not just with head."

I felt myself becoming agitated. Did I wish with all my being? Or was it just an idea I'd had? Perhaps the System, as Mr. Ouspensky calls it, was no more than a handful of "ideas" that had no real bearing upon the predicament of real people. Perhaps it was effective for certain people, but not for others, in other words, not for the likes of KM.

Mr. Gurdjieff leaned toward me and touched the arm of my chair.

"We watch together," he said. "Perhaps we learn something..."

Automatically, I turned to look at the people who were working. What can one learn if one is not able to participate? The thought entered my mind, but failed to take hold. It was as if one part of me wanted to rage and stamp its feet and bemoan my incapacity to run about like the members of the scurry party, whereas another part, the part now in possession of my faculties, was unimpressed. There was something reassuring in Gurdjieff's watchful presence, in his words. Perhaps we learn something. It appeared to me all of a sudden that the most important thing was to be watchful, to pay attention to what was going on around me.

I sat there with my hands resting in my lap. The wood was in deep shade, shot through with shafts of sunlight. When the people who were working in the shade passed through the sunlight, they seemed to fuse with the light and disappear. But if I looked at the patches of sunlight, I could see people only in flashes as they traversed the light. I did not cease to be aware of Gurdjieff's presence, but I no longer felt ill at ease with the silence between us, nor was I troubled by questions that I could not formulate.

"Davolna!" called out Mr. Gurdjieff at length. "Enough!"

He beckoned with his arms, and the members of the scurry party gathered around us, throwing themselves on the ground, wiping perspiring brows, some of them breathing hard. I felt myself suddenly exposed, sitting above the recumbent group, next to Mr. Gurdjieff. Perhaps I was afraid that he would take it into his head to make an example of me in some way. But there was no help for it.

Someone asked a question about freedom. I did not catch what was said. Mr. Gurdjieff replied that there are two kinds of freedom, but that we need only concern ourselves with the lesser of the two: freedom from inner slavery. There are innumerable influences that keep us in slavery; to wage war against each of them individually would take a score of lifetimes. Therefore, we must identify our chief enemies and work only against these for a time.

"What are they called," he asked, "these enemies, these representatives of the devil? They are called Madame Vanity and Monsieur Self-Love."

He leaned forward in his chair, still in the same erect posture, and looked around the group. His smile was of a peculiar, almost provocative nature. It was as though he had mentioned the names of two persons with whom each of us was associated in a private and shameful way.

"How to master them? you are wondering. I am not vain, you say, certainly not so vain as other people, but all the same, may be something in what he says. I do not love myself any more than Jack or Jill, but on the other hand, am not a saint. How can I be better, purer in mind, kinder in thought and deed to others? How can I be a saint?"

He paused again to look around him. His smile broadened, then in an instant disappeared.

"Personally I advise not to waste time with thoughts of this kind, but to reason directly and actively with self."

He leaped to his feet and strode across the clearing, making for a log upon which sat two of the Russian students, a tall attractive young woman and a middle-aged scholarly man with a pair of steel-rimmed spectacles on the end of his nose. They were sitting close together, and Mr. Gurdjieff approached as though he intended to bowl them both over. They parted hastily and settled on opposite ends of the log, while Mr. Gurdjieff seated himself in the place they had jointly occupied. He took up the same posture, one hand on his knee, the fingers of the other dangling loosely, stared over our heads for a moment, and then crouched down dramatically and darted furtive glances at the pair whom he had so abruptly separated. His expression of commingled fear and malice was so convincing that a ripple of inadvertent laughter went through the group.

"I am sitting here between Mademoiselle Verotchka and Monsieur Ognyov," he proclaimed. "We live together in this place. Now suppose I overhear Mademoiselle Verotchka tell Monsieur Ognyov I am a fool. Is always unpleasant to hear such thing. Ach!" he exclaimed, shaking his shoulders and twisting himself this way and that, as though in an attempt to rid himself of something that clung to him. "Better not to hear! But once you hear, is no help. V tells O I am a fool, my 'degree of culture' is not equal to his, he must not believe a word I say. All this I overhear—so much the worse for me. At once I am hurt and offended. I discover V's opinion matters to me, something I did not know before. I think and think about V and walk around not knowing where I am. I forget myself for a long time."

The extraordinary thing was that the little drama he had asked us to imagine seemed to be playing itself out before our eyes. The tall woman looked quite discomfited, as though she had in reality said something disparaging about Gurdjieff to her companion. She sat with her hands clasped nervously together, her proud and aristocratic head tilted to one side, staring off into the branches of the trees. Her companion sat hunched over, his larger head bowed, ample belly hanging between his knees, motionless. And Gurdjieff's face had actually assumed an aggrieved expression. The grievance could also be heard in his voice. Its sour tone set my teeth on edge; for a moment I was afraid that we were about to have an unpleasant scene. Then I happened to look at Dr. Young, who was sitting cross-legged on the ground a few feet away from my chair. He gave me a meaningful look and deliberately closed one eye.

"So with everyone all the time," Gurdjieff said sharply. "We three are not special, though perhaps we like to believe. We cease to think of one person who offends us. Another gets our goat, as is said."

The speed and ease of the transformation from self-indulgent brooding to self-possessed provocateur, was stunning. It was a remarkable theatrical performance, but I felt it was more than the mere juggling of roles. When Gurdjieff had assumed the aggrieved expression and tone, I had been utterly convinced that he was about to lose his self-possession. But I was aware, too, that this representation of grievance, of anguished and futile preoccupation with the opinion of others, resonated with something in me. It was as if he had given a representation, not of his own inner state, but of mine. I looked around uneasily, wondering if the other members of the group were having similar reactions to the performance.

"Well, Mademoiselle V believes I am a fool," Gurdjieff resumed. "Is good. Why should I be offended? I reason with self as follows. If she calls me fool, does this mean she is wise? I can see she acts like child. When she needs to take decision, she asks everyone she meets, even cab driver. And then she does the last thing she hears—or what she wants, without reflecting, without remembering what was said. Is this the way of wise person? As for my 'degree of culture,' may be her mother teach her to look down on all others and therefore she cannot help. I know I am not a fool, I am I, and I have good reason to do what I do. If a fool calls me fool, why should I take it to heart, as is said?"

The tall woman had turned the upper part of her body away from Gurdjieff, as though trying to efface herself where she sat. The man's head sagged lower between his fleshy shoulders.

"On the other hand—may be I act like a fool! In that case, I should thank her. Now I *see* I act like a fool. I want to see. Therefore I am not offended."

"As for Ognyov"—the man's body gave a little involuntary jerk—"suppose he gives me a dirty look. Do I allow to upset me? May be is not intended for me. May be he is thinking of dear Mama, or he eats too much Khaizarian bastourma. Or someone tells him I do not change socks every day, or forget to bathe.

He changes his opinion of me. So much the worse for *him*. I am sorry he looks through another's eyes, cannot look for self. I pity because he cannot hide what he thinks, even though he does not wish to show. But I am not offended. Have too much pride."

As he said the word pride, he appeared to take a deep breath. His cheeks became fuller, his shoulders swelled, and his entire body seemed to become heavier and more substantial. The shrinking, crouching figure of a moment before was replaced by a larger-than-life Gurdjieff. His feet were planted firmly, his head erect, his elbow thrust forward. He looked like someone bracing himself to receive a blow with complete confidence in his power to withstand it. And as I watched, a certain expression crept across his face, an expression of smug self-satisfaction that recalled the phrase "swollen with pride." This gave me a little shock. The man sitting before me was swollen with pride. This was not what I had expected to see.

And yet it was possible to see something else too, as though the mask of pride did not cover the entire face. It was a disguise, and a strangely ineffective one. From behind the mask of his play-acting, another looked out, the dispassionate observer whom I had encountered in the Café de la Paix, the student of human nature who had asked me to "tell about parents" and then sat back to observe the results. He waved his pride to distract us, as the magician uses the movement of his hands to distract the audience from the trick that underlies his magic, but all the time he was watching us, to see if—what? I do not know. To see if any of us would tumble to it? To see if any one of us could catch the slight of hand and perceive how the trick was turned?

It was at this moment that one of the English students, a man with a refined accent and mincing intonation, chose to ask a question:

"What is the difference between the greater and the lesser freedom?"

The figure swollen with pride abruptly disappeared. Mr. Gurdjieff was himself again, at least the self that I was most familiar with. He whirled about to face the direction from which the question came.

"Bah!" he exclaimed, slapping his open palm upon his thigh. "You hear about possibility of freedom from inner enemies and you want something else, you want more information, more fact. For what? The greater freedom is freedom from external influences, from accident, illness, death. Which of us can be free from these things? May be struggle with Madame Vanity and Monsieur Self-Love not difficult enough for you. Perhaps your *pride*"—the word came off his tongue virtually dripping with sarcasm—"will not allow you to undertake. So you look for something impossible, something that will make you 'noble failure,' 'if-only' man, 'should-have' man."

I did not see the man who asked the question. He was in the shadow of a tree—or perhaps his mortification caused the ground to open and swallow him. Gurdjieff got to his feet and walked slowly, placing his feet deliberately, back to the chair beside me. He turned, took in the group with a glance, and sat down. He continued to sit for some time, looking at the ground, before he spoke.

"Pride is our chief enemy," he said in a voice so quiet that I could see people at the back of the group leaning forward to catch his words. "Pride is great obstacle to all our wishes, the weapon of Madame Vanity, Monsieur Self-Love. And yet—without pride man can do nothing. Pride is sign: he who has is of heaven, he who has is already half-free. Pride is heaven; pride is hell. But how are we to tell false pride from real, dirty thing from pure, cock on dunghill from bird of prey?"

He paused and looked around again. A sly smile crept across his face; he seemed on the verge of another of his extraordinary transformations.

"Thank Heaven, I hear you say, does not apply to me. That I am sitting here shows I have only real pride. Do not have to look for false pride in self; is something to see in others."

He made an abrupt gesture in the air with his hand, as though dispelling his own sarcasm. People rose from the ground and began to straggle off across the lawn toward the chateau in twos and threes. The tall woman and the portly man who had provided Gurdjieff with the pretext for his little drama walked together, leaning toward one another, as though for support. I looked around nervously for Patrick. Gurdjieff caught my eye.

"After eat, digest," he informed me. "No?"

He placed his hands upon his belly, which looked suddenly distended, as though he had just finished a large meal. He closed his eyes and allowed his chin to rest upon his chest. In a moment I detected the sound of a snore.

I felt that I had in fact been given a great deal of food for thought, but I found myself quite unable to think about it. I seemed to be entirely confined to the present moment, unable to enter my thoughts of the past or the future. Though keenly aware of the slumped form in the chair beside me, I could not even ask myself whether or not he was actually sleeping. I watched myself trying to think, about freedom lesser and greater, about Madame Vanity and Monsieur Self-Love; my attention was not engaged. Would I be able to remember what Mr. Gurdjieff had said? But there was something almost laughable in the thought that I should go to my room and write down as much as I could recall, as I knew many of the others were hastening to do. It was useless. All that mattered was the play of light and shade in the now silent garden, the life warm and vibrant within my body: me, here, now.

A tremendous belch made me start forward in the chair. Mr. Gurdjieff was looking at me with large startled eyes. There was something so utterly ingenuous in his look, since he could not possibly have expected me to believe that he had thus woken himself up. He sighed heavily and got to his feet, stooping a little, as though suddenly old. But his face was lit up by his brilliant, child-like smile.

"Now rest?" he suggested, as he moved away. "Will send Patreek."

I watched him emerge from the trees and start across the lawn. He shambled a little and swayed from side to side, as though he were unwell. But I had just seen him move about like a cat ready to pounce. More play-acting—but to what end?

I must have closed my eyes for a few moments. When I opened them, he was no longer in sight.

What a strange adventure I have embarked on. That such a life should be for me.

28 October

Olgivanna—with a bunch of flowers, asters, turtlehead, and some pale leggy sunflowers.

"How lovely! But where did you get them?"

"Stolen from under the eagle eyes of Miss Madison! For your sake I have become a criminal."

"I hope she did not see you," I said. "She will bear a tale to Mr. Gurdjieff."

"It will have been worth it just to see you smile like that. Besides, the frost will carry off all her flowers before long."

She disliked Miss Madison. I had formed a very negative impression of Miss Madison myself. I frequently imagined that I would ask her to be nicer to Patrick, though I knew that I would never dare to do so.

"Thank you," I said. "I will try to deserve them. And torture will not wring from me how I came by them."

I sat on the bed and leaned back against the pillows. She settled herself in her chair beside the fire and smiled up at me. I had been hoping she would come.

"Olgivanna," I said. "Why is it that I cannot make my peace with my father? Within myself, I mean. Our relationship has been formed by all that has gone before, and there is no changing it, not at this stage, not even if I had the time and the resolve. But why is it that I cannot be at peace with my own feelings?"

"What are those feelings, Katherine?" she said.

"You have been good enough to sit up with me and to allow me to speak about my family and about my life in New Zealand. I can see that you are tired. I must let you go to bed. Perhaps I will sleep too. I feel as if I could."

She sat up a little straighter in her chair, lifted the rope of her hair from off her shoulders and let it fall again. Her face was rosy in the firelight. Her eyes shone with sympathy. How comforting her presence was. I did *not* want to let her go. Not yet.

"Tell me again," she said. "But this time—tell all. Do not hold anything back."

What had I held back? I had told her the whole story, how my father had seemed to encourage my early literary aspirations, how he had taken a covert pride in having his daughter a writer (or so it seemed to me), how I had managed to persuade him to send me back to London where I was to make a name for myself and become a credit to my family and my country. Instead of which I promptly fell from grace and required to be rescued, to be whisked away ignominiously to Bavaria, where I lost my child in secret. How thereafter I affected to be above the judgment of my family—I *have* no family, I would say, save Jack and me—how this was no more successful than my half-hearted attempts to *please* my father. The more he seemed to distance himself from me, the more I looked forward to his infrequent visits with excitement and hope, but no matter how pleasant they had been—and they were invariably *pleasant*, nothing if not *pleasant!*—I was left with a sense of disappointment, as though some unarticulated longing had been unfulfilled.

It suddenly occurred to me that this was not the whole story, that I had never told the whole story to anyone, except perhaps to Jack, and even Jack, to his sorrow, was now an actor in the drama rather than a member of the audience. Was there something in the story, a critical duplicity, a staunch refusal to see, that was now plain to Olgivanna, but hidden from myself? I began to feel afraid.

Olgivanna must have sensed my confusion. She leaned toward me and touched my hand lightly.

"Tell how you feel, dear. First on the one side, then the other. Do not leave anything out. Above all, do not judge yourself. I will not judge you. Trust me."

"Do you mean how I feel for and against? My feelings of love and duty—and my anger, my sense of betrayal."

"That is just what I mean."

"First, love," I said. "My father was the great Pa-man of my childhood, the arbiter of all taste, the king of the castle, whose going and coming were the great events of the day, who bore the whole household on his Olympian shoulders, who was winning and wise and—perfect, albeit he took himself a little too seriously, in the tacit opinion of the women of the household. My father seemed on a par with God, a rather distant and preoccupied God, whose direct influence did not extend to the remote sphere in which we children lived, whose intervention could not be counted upon to rescue us from our small tribulations, but whose appearance nevertheless was as constant and as regular as the sun's. The child in me still regards him in this way.

"Then, duty: there is my indebtedness toward him, which can never be repaid; that is my great sin. I must always be at fault in regard to him because I insisted and importuned, I made myself intolerable to my family until I had gained my end—and then I went off to behave quite horribly in spite of all my promises. My great desire has been to win my father's love anew. I had it as a child—I must have had it!—but once forfeited, it seems I can never get it back. To all appearances, he has forgiven me—oh, not in so many words, he left that up to Mother—but really he has lost interest, he is no longer listening, and yet I still yearn to be a dutiful daughter, to return his kindness (for he has been very kind, you know, and continues to make me an allowance, which he is not obliged to do), to win his admiration for my work, not his critical admiration, but the pride one takes in the work of a daughter, just because it is one's own daughter. No, it is more than that: I wish for him to see me, just once, to *see* me, not as a dutiful or prodigal daughter, not as an invalid, certainly, not even as a writer, but simply as the person I am, nothing added, nothing taken away. But it is useless ...

I paused to try to gain possession of myself.

"And the other side," Olgivanna murmured.

"Since I have been ill, it has been harder," I said. "Once the defenses are fallen between you and Death, everything touches you on the raw. There is the wretched pittance of an allowance for which I am obliged to be grateful. His affectation of having made a great sacrifice for my sake, of having to deprive himself, when in fact he is a moderately wealthy man. Oh! money, how I hate it, the lack of it, the excess of it. But if he had been able to see how ill I was and to really help me, it might have made a difference. There is the disregard of my work: my literary accomplishments count for naught—as though my sisters had accomplished a great deal just by getting married to men who support them in the style of the class to which they belong, whereas I have supported *myself*. While I was still able to work I produced two and three reviews a week, and I have been obliged to spend more time reviewing than writing. But it is at bottom my father's conviction that Jack should support me. No one could possibly work harder than Jack—or be recompensed so poorly for it. My father has never regarded Jack as a real husband; he is simply the one who chose to make an honest woman of me. As far as my family is concerned, I have married badly, I should have chosen someone more like my father: the mercantile type, bluff, hearty, hail-fellow-well-met, with a fund of unrepeatable jokes who must regard Jack with instinctive distrust, as the ineffectual literary man who is incapable of acting in or upon the world, the man of ideas, who spends most of his time in cloud-cuckoo land..."

I paused for breath. I felt thoroughly ashamed of myself, to have violated the privacy of my family and divulged our most unflattering secrets to a complete stranger. But I was determined to follow Olgivanna's prompting and to spit it out. And then I could scarcely help myself: something within me was roused.

"A number of years ago I sent my father one of my stories. He acknowledged that he had received it, as one acknowledges a greeting card. Very well. But later I learned that he had read it—and "chucked it behind the fireplace," as it had, in his opinion, a very disreputable narrator. "It wasn't even clever," was his final judgment.

"So I have disgraced the family on all fronts. My personal affairs have been in disarray, I have been unable to find myself a husband capable of supporting me, and I have chosen to associate myself with the artistic element, which carries, in my father's mind, a certain whiff of immorality. The least I could have done under the circumstances is to write in what he would regard as a clever manner. But no! I wasn't even capable of that!"

The tears came to my eyes. It was too much for me. I felt that I must not allow myself to become upset, if only for the sake of my health. And if I could not master my grief, I would be obliged to send Olgivanna away, to order to weep in secret. Even Jack had only seen my anger, not my grief. I was overcome by shame.

But when I looked at Olgivanna, expecting to see my own self-loathing reflected in her eyes, she was sitting with quiet composure, completely detached, waiting for me to continue. Her eyes held mine easily: they were quietly encouraging. I know how hard this is, they seemed to say, but it is *necessary*.

"Oh! Olgivanna," I cried. "My hatred! My hatred! Will I never be rid of it? To hate the simple ruddy health of people I sit down to eat with—because they are healthy and can come and go as they please—and I cannot! To hate as I hate—my friend Ida in Ospedaletti, my sisters for their comfortable marriages and prejudices, my mother for her refusal to hear my confession, my father for his indifference to the gift of my work that I would make him. To hate one's family because one has never been *seen* by them, never acknowledged for what one is, but always it has been, Why are you not like such-and-such a person? Why do you have this wish and not that? Why do you not resemble the child that I want you to be?"

I found myself gasping for air. I paused to breathe as deeply as I could, to try to calm myself.

"I do not know if you have ever hated anyone, if you know what it is like. Hate is the *other* passion. It has all the opposite effects of Love. It is my deadly deadly enemy, and when it has got me in its grip, it fills me with death and corruption, it makes me feel soiled, irredeemably soiled. Just as the one is Light, so the other is Darkness. God! It is like being under a curse. And the worst of it is that it never spends itself, is never exhausted, but simply withdraws like a snake and remains silently coiled within me until it is called forth again. Oh, Olgivanna. What am I do to? What is the use of my being here? I am bad, bad, and I cannot be good. And I have so little time."

I was at this moment filled from top to toe with self-pity. And yet a part of me stood aside from this emotion. That part suddenly remembered Mr. Gurdjieff's words about becoming a saint: *Personally I advise you not to waste your time...*

"It is that way with all strong emotions," Olgivanna said. "With everything, really. They come and go."

"But when they are present—I am lost!"

"That is because I identify myself with them. I become the emotion, anger or fear or whatever it may be. Nothing of myself remains."

"How true that is," I said. "But what is to be done?"

She looked away from me for a moment, staring out the tall window at the night, a wry smile playing about her beautiful lips.

"I think that St. George did not really slay the dragon," she said brightly. "You can see this in some of the old pictures. He subdued it, but did not kill it because it cannot be killed—and because he needed its energy. You cannot kill that snake of yours, and you must not try. It is a part of you. It appears repulsive to you only because it is uncontrolled. You must not allow it to eat you alive, to poison your relations with people and with yourself. But neither must you shut it away in a closed room and pretend that it has died."

"I understand what you are saying, but I do not know what I must do."

"It is more a question of what you must *not* do. You must bide your time until the snake emerges, and then you must make use of the opportunity. You may suffer because of its presence, and yet you must not bid it leave you or let it sink its teeth into those around you. It is a very fine line you must walk. And you must expect to fail—many, many times. We have all of us fallen from grace repeatedly. It is one thing to forgive others, but we must learn to forgive ourselves."

There was something in what she said that gave me ease. But I did not like the sound of her many, many times. It reminded me—as everything does, eventually—that my own time is so short.

"How can I use the time that remains to me? I do not expect to see my father again."

She glanced at me quickly and then looked away. I thought I saw a glint of tears in her eyes. A lump rose in my throat. I did not wish to let all go to smash, even in the presence of such a sympathetic person as Olgivanna.

"I am a passionate and outspoken person," she said smiling, "who must be careful to hold her tongue. But I have learned that I must handle others gently, not only when I am with them, but when I am alone. What is the use, as Shakespeare puts it, to smile and smile, if on the inside you are a villain, seething with rage?" (She glanced at me girlishly, to see if I had appreciated her allusion.) "What is the use of being polite in someone's presence when later in private you commit murder, mentally, and tear the person limb from limb."

"I am guilty of all that and more," I said, virtually beside myself again. "But I am helpless in the face of it. What am I to *do*?"

"Yes, we are helpless," she murmured. "And yet there is something we can do. What if you had never heard of this work? Then you could treat people just as you liked, in public and in private; you would have no reason to do otherwise. For some few—certainly for you, Katherine—there comes a time when this does not suffice. Then it becomes necessary to take up arms against your deadly enemy, to say No to your unpleasant thoughts and feelings. Something in me wants to yield to them, to revel in them, to say Yes. But I see that it will not do. You have undertaken this struggle. Sometimes you have been successful, sometimes not. Sometimes one emphatic No! will banish the unpleasantness. Sometimes it is necessary to persist. And sometimes, as you have seen, your deadly enemy cannot be made to yield, No cannot wrestle Yes to the ground, they remained locked in an inconclusive struggle—or No is swept away and all is lost."

Again I grew calm under the influence of her voice. I sensed the presence of an inner life that I had only just begun to touch in myself. Olgivanna continued:

"The struggle of Yes or No is all very well and good, as my English governess used to say, but it is only a partial view of things: Yes *or* No, black *or* white, good *or* bad. My father sits on the right side of God." (She chuckled at her own conceit.) "My father is hateful and low. This is the language of children—and yet how few of us outgrow it! What is required is not Yes *or* No, but Yes *and* No, a point of view that can embrace contraries, that can embrace Light *and* Dark and mix them to produce an entirely new thing. This is a very different kind of struggle from that of Yes *or* No. It requires both more strength and more restraint, for it allows this new thing, which is neither Yes nor No, but higher than these, to enter in."

She stopped with a little shrug and clapped her hands together sharply.

"I've talked for too long!" she exclaimed. "I hope you will forgive me. It is something that can only be truly known by experience."

"I am very grateful to you for what you *have* said," I told her, sincerely, but with a sinking feeling, because I knew that I would shortly be left alone with my thoughts. "Perhaps it is something like what Mr. Gurdjieff means when he says that one must love one's parents with an objective love."

"Perhaps it is!" Olgivanna said, rising from her place. "But I want to tell you this. I can see that you, Katherine, are making a very sincere effort to put things right in your relations with your father. Such an effort is never wasted. And it can have far-reaching effects. Your father will be aware of it, even if he never acknowledges it."

This defied common sense, and yet it intrigued me. She touched my shoulder lightly and went to the door.

"You will sleep now," she said, smiling. "I can tell."

As she opened the door, I had a moment of weakness.

"Olgivanna," I said. "It is very kind of you to spend so much time with me. Were you also assigned to me by Mr. Gurdjieff, just as Patrick and Adèle have been?"

"Yes," she said gaily. "He told me that there was an Englishwoman who was very sick and that I was to take very good care of her."

She was happy, and then she saw how it struck me. That she only came because she was *assigned*. That her concern and her patience had been *work*.

"That it would be a very good thing for my soul," she persisted, serious now, almost solemn.

"I'm grateful," I said, pulling myself together.

"As am I."

She went out and closed the door after her, slowly, and sadly, as it seemed.

What a way to repay kindness, Katherine. Strive to be good. Strive to be better.

I sat for a moment in the fading warmth of the fireplace.

Nay, said another voice. Strive to accept.

29 October

Patrick did not come for my chair on the day of the scurry party, and eventually I had wandered back to the house by myself. I did not see him until the following day, and then he seemed to be avoiding me. I called to him from my place at the table, but he was on kitchen duty and could not pause even for a moment. It rained, and I did not go out of doors.

Later, in my room, too fagged to go down to the dancing, feeling abandoned by all the world, specifically by Jack, my Pa, Orage, and Olgivanna, entirely cast away and alone with the pain in my heart and my fear and the coiled serpent of my hatred.

Comes a knock to the door. Enter a disheveled Patrick, wet hair dripping across his eyes.

"I'm sorry, Mrs. Murry," were the first words out of his mouth.

"About what, Patrick?"

"About your chair."

"I didn't need it today, Patrick."

"It was out all night and got drenched in the rain. So did Mr. Gurdjieff's chair. Matters, I mean, Miss Madison, says they are ruined."

"Oh dear," I said. "It's my fault. I should have remembered to tell somebody they were out."

"Miss Madison says it's *my* fault. I am the chair-carrier. She said for me to come and apologize to you."

"Oh, but surely—"

"I'm sorry, Mrs. Murry. Now I have to go."

He backed away toward the door, reaching behind him for the handle. My heart sank. I did not want to be left alone. I tried to think of something that would not simply be the kind of typical question that well-meaning adults ask children.

"When is your aunt coming to see you, Patrick?"

He stopped, squirmed a little, lifted his hand and brushed the wet hair out of his eyes, then held it clamped to the crown of his head, staring off at the wall behind me.

"I don't know."

"Does she come to see you often?"

"I don't want to see her," he blurted out. "She says that my mother will never be well."

Good Lord, I said to myself. What a thing to say to a child. It occurred to me that I was wrong to press him.

"Anyway, she'll just spend all her time talking to Mr. Gurdjieff," he said. "That's what she always does when she comes."

I was stymied. I felt acutely conscious of my own inadequacy. Perhaps it was just as well that I had never had a child. But surely I could do better than Patrick's aunt. To have dumped him on Mr. Gurdjieff like this and to spend so little time with him.

"Do you have any grandparents, Patrick?

"When my mother got sick, she left me with my grandfather. I liked to be with him. But then he had a stroke and died."

"Patrick!"

He gave me a cool inquisitive glance, as if to say, "What are *you* so upset about?"

"I still talk to him," he explained. "Even though he's not there anymore. It's just like he *is* there really. He told me before he died that dead people are just like anybody else, except they get very tired and have to rest a lot and then they don't say anything when you talk to them. But sometimes they do say things. You just have to listen very hard to hear them."

He was watching me carefully. I did not know what to say.

"Do you believe in dead people, Mrs. Murry? That they're not really dead, I mean."

This question was obviously of great import to Patrick. He was waiting intently upon my answer. I started to tell him I used to believe—and the words stuck in my throat! How awful to think that I had not remembered my beloved brother in such a very long time! I was afraid to think how long. If it had not been for Patrick, I would not have thought of him at all.

"I had a brother whom I loved dearly, Patrick. He was my little brother. I still miss him a great deal. You remind me of him, a little."

"What happened to him?"

"He died in the War."

"I'm sorry, Mrs. Murry," he said simply, and quite without embarrassment.

"Thank you, Patrick. It seems a long time ago. It *is* a long time ago since we were children together..."

I can hardly credit that it was a part of my life. When I saw Chummie for the last time, he was so sure he would come back; I was so sure with him. And then we were to go back to New Zealand together and find everything—just as we remembered it. Do you remember, Katie? he would say. Of that conviction, of that star-struck plan, of my very grief, what remains? No, I no longer believe. What can we do for the dead, for *our* dead? Nothing. How terrible that answer is!

The poor child was standing there, looking at me in amazement. I had an inspiration.

"Come here and let me dry your hair. You'll catch your death going about with a wet head. I know all about such things— being an invalid!"

He stepped forward involuntarily to the bed, and I seized a towel, draped it over his long dank locks, and rubbed his head as vigorously as I could between my hands. He submitted without a word, but when I tried to complete the treatment with a hug, he edged away.

"Thank you," he muttered.

To my horror I saw that his eyes had filled with tears.

"Patrick! What is the matter?"

"Miss Madison has killed Ptolemy!" he burst out.

"Good Lord! What can you mean?"

"She caught him among her flowers and wrung his neck," he wailed. "And now she is going to serve him for dinner!"

There followed a storm of weeping. He fell to his knees and thrust his face against the side of the bed. I let him cry until I could sit still no longer. Then I put my hand on his shoulder. He slid away from my hand as soon as he became aware of it. But he accepted a handkerchief and dabbed at his face with it.

"Tell me what happened," I insisted. "From the beginning, please."

It transpired that in spite of Patrick's best efforts to repair the pen, the chickens had escaped, and by the time he arrived on the scene Miss Madison had laid hands on one of them and made good her promise. Then she had reported him to Mr. Gurdjieff.

"And what does Mr. Gurdjieff have to say about this?" I demanded to know.

Patrick squirmed a little as though he did not want to answer. But I was insistent. I really wished to know how Gurdjieff had dealt with the situation.

"He says I should not have destroyed Miss Madison's favorite delphinium."

"Oh, Patrick!"

"He says the chicken can be eaten, but the plant is no longer any use. He says I should not have climbed the wall and gone to Avon. Miss Madison has made a rule that anyone who wants to leave the Prieuré must ask her for permission, and everyone is supposed to obey her. But there are too many rules since she is in charge. I can't follow *all* of them."

"And what did he say to Miss Madison?" I asked indignantly.

"He says that she had no business to kill Ptolemy, who was *his* chicken, not hers or mine."

This sounded even-handed enough, but it was hardly the wisdom of Solomon, and I was disappointed.

"Is that all?"

Patrick hesitated, then burst out:

"He says we both have failed. I am supposed to obey Miss Madison, and she is supposed to be director and not to annoy him with unimportant problems like a dead chicken."

"I suppose he is a busy man, Patrick," I said weakly.

"After he sent Miss Madison away, he asked me if I had learned anything. I didn't know what I was supposed to learn! He says I must learn to live with what he calls the unpleasant manifestations of others. He says I have to be conscious and not just to react. I don't understand."

"Maybe you will understand when you are a little older, Patrick."

Patrick glared at me out of his fine gray eyes, and I was afraid he was going to run out of the room. But then a sly smile curled the corners of his mouth.

"That's just what he says himself, Mrs. Murry."

"Then it must be true," I said, smiling back at him. "Great minds think alike."

He began to edge toward the door.

"Do you like it here, Patrick?"

"I like Mr. Gurdjieff," he asserted, sticking out his jaw a little, as though answering an implied criticism.

"What do you like about him?"

"He tells me what he wants from me," came the answer without hesitation. "No one else will tell me, not my father or my aunt or Miss Madison—or you!"

His response gave me a little shock of guilt. I was sitting up in bed, and he was standing by the door, as though waiting to be dismissed. I did not feel like detaining him any more. I had kept him long enough—against his will. The feeling of loneliness and isolation started to come over me again.

"Good night, Patrick," I said. "Thank you for coming."

I looked down at the covers. When I looked up, I was surprised to find him still standing there.

"Do you have any children, Mrs. Murry?"

"No, Patrick."

"I'm sorry."

"So am I, Patrick. Run along now. I want you to find me a new chair for tomorrow. I would like to be out of doors if I can. You must not fail, do you hear me?"

He grinned—and fled. What would he have said if I'd told him that up until a few years ago I had had a little child, aged seven and a half, of indeterminate sex, an imaginary child, the only kind I am capable of taking care of? It was born of those long sleepless nights at the Casetta when the ocean roared and whimpered like a living thing in pain and empty days when I was too weak to work and lay beside the stove while the infernal wind chased round the house. Sometimes it was a little girl, to whom I confided all my thoughts (those that were fit for childish ears). Then for a long time it had very often been a boy, the little boy of my letter to Jack, who accompanied me to England and thence to Randogne. There I let him go; it was the end of the dream. He would now be just about Patrick's age, if I had kept him...

30 X 22
Le Prieuré

Father dear,

Do you remember one night before I left New Zealand for the last time and returned to London to make my life there, for better or for worse? I had been disagreeable to everyone during dinner and had finally brought Vera to tears with my sarcastic remarks and flounced out of the room. Oh, I am so dreadfully bored, had been my constant refrain—for months. But the truth of the matter is that I was on the verge of a nervous collapse: I could not sleep, and I was in despair. You came quietly into the room where I lay face down on my bed, pretending to be asleep. I knew it was you from the way your shoes squeaked, the comfortable old shoes that you wore about the house, that you refused to part with, though everyone joked about them and tried to steal them away from you. What would the customers of the National Bank say if they knew what kind of shoes the manager wears at home? But I remember that every muscle in my body tensed as you approached. I was expecting that reprimand that I knew I richly deserved—for my behavior had been inexcusable—but I also knew that I simply could not bear it. I was virtually mad with frustration and self-reproach. You stood beside the bed for a moment, and I held my breath, feeling that something was about to break inside me, something rare and fragile that could never be restored. Then, to my astonishment, I felt your hand upon the small of my back. It was so unexpected that I experienced it as a sort of shock. You didn't stroke me as you occasionally used to do when I was a child of five or six and I'd sidled up to where you sprawled in your after-work chair on the verandah, along with the rest of your boisterous brood. You simply let your hand rest there, and I felt something pass from you to me, a kind of electricity. Then you murmured, as though to yourself, There comes a time in every life when a body can't sleep. I shouldn't worry about it if I were you, Kass. I didn't move. I didn't say anything. But I heard. Then you took your hand away and left the room. My body felt tremendously heavy and tired, as though you had somehow contrived to drain all the nervous energy out of it. I slept.

It was precisely the right gesture, Father, the right thing to say. It was a moment of light and understanding in the misery of the unconscious struggle in which I was engaged. It lifted me out of myself. It gave me back to myself. I was grateful for it, though I could not find a way to say so. I am still grateful for it after all these years. It remains in my mind as a symbol of what "home" means, of what one hopes and expects to find there, and I thank you for it.

And now: something that you will *not* be pleased to hear. I have tried to persuade myself that it did not need to be said. But I do not expect to live for very much longer, and this has made certain things clear to me. You have continued to be generous to me in the matter of my allowance. Had I been well, three hundred pounds a year would have seemed a princely sum. But consumption is a debilitating illness. I have lost the ability to earn a living and been forced to pinch pennies and to live from hand to mouth—and on occasion to accept money from people to whom I did not wish to reveal my need. All of which I could accept—save for the knowledge that you could have relieved my distress and did not *choose* to do so. Oh! tell me that this is not so! Tell me that you didn't realize the extremity of my need. Tell me anything but that my sin is still unforgiven and that "home" does not receive and cherish me.

That is all in the past. I am very well looked after here, and as for my straitened circumstances, I do not think that even the most expensive treatment would have made any difference; it seems that from the first it was only a matter of time. But I would have known you loved me as I knew it in the long ago when you came to my room and put your hand on my back—and restored me to the living. For surely I am a person worthy of forgiveness, in spite of all. What can a Father do if he cannot forgive?

And then there is the matter of my work. No doubt you think it impertinent of me to mention it—but it galls me so. I do not care a whit whether you like it or not. It is not all that I would make it, shall never be now, but it is what I have done, it contains an aspiration and a longing that are better than what it is in itself. Can you not take pride in it because of what it might be? Can you not take pride in it because it has its true source and inspiration in the life of my family and in New Zealand? Can you not take pride in it just because it is mine?

Enough. Let me tell you something else I remember from the time before I went away. We were walking by the bay one day, you and I, improbably alone together, and you were polishing an apple on your sleeve. Do you see this apple? you said to me. Where in the wide world would you find an apple as fine? This is the sort of incomparable thing that this country can produce. There was such feeling in your voice, such pride. I felt entirely at one with you. I knew just what you meant. There was something of the essence of New Zealand in that apple, something of the soil that has nourished you and me in turn. It gives me a little thrill to think of it. You see, I say to myself, we understand each other after all. I love and honor that essence. It is what I will strive from now on to express in my writing, if I am spared.

God bless you, Father.

Ever your loving and grateful child,
Kass

1 November

My family—my real family—is a family of the dead: Grandma, Chummie, Mother. I have been thinking a great deal of Grandma lately. It is important to think of one's dead, one's beloved dead. Where is that photograph of Grandma that Mother gave me at a time when she still loved me? It is my own dear Grandma, young and lovely. She is leaning against her husband's shoulder, her hair parted meekly, her eyes raised. Her arm and shoulder. The sleeve of her dress. Her dear hands. The velvet ribbon. How I long for this photograph. I *must* see it again.

Nor do I have with me a photograph of Chummie. But I *will* remember. That I *can* do. Where is there to be found in life a love as pure as that we can have for the dead, who make no demands, who are still and utterly silent, who utter no cry of protest when we cease to be mindful of them. If after all we continue to love them, surely it is with a different kind of love, a love that is not of this world, a love that can *let be...*

As I pass the door of one of the large common rooms, the sound of Mr. Gurdjieff's voice arrests me:

"Ordinary person makes demand that life and the world should satisfy every need."

I pause in the doorway. He is sitting in an armchair by the window, the center of a group of some two dozen people whom I do not know. He is leaning forward, speaking with intensity, looking at each person in turn.

"Ordinary person, he thinks what he wants is reasonable, proper. But is impossible that the world should be organized to please him. Since he gives all his energy to impossible demand, all his energy is eaten by disappointment."

I leaned against the door jamb. I was tired. I wished to lie down. But the voice was like a source of nourishment from which I could not tear myself away.

"No one comes to this work who is not disappointed. But most will never know—What is the itch that disturbs them? They scratch in different ways—money, food, sex. Spoil their lives: still they do not see. Build castles in Spain, as is said, or blame Mama and Papa, the world, God, for not giving what little child wants. This work not for everyone. People prefer dream to disappointment, prefer to attempt impossible. This work *almost* impossible, but for disappointed person—is the only thing *really* possible."

He paused. A faint smile appeared. When he spoke again, it was softly, almost to himself.

"One who is disappointed in favorite dream, who is tired of old life, who has lost taste for suffering and self-pity. For such one, when there is no hope, then at last—there is hope."

He turned his head, and our eyes met. He held my eyes easily, casually, in the manner of a friend who does not yet know what he wishes to say, but trusts that you will not take it amiss.

"Not for you," he said at length.

All heads turned toward the doorway. I felt something cold creeping over my limbs. I could not move.

"This talk not for you," he said. "You not waste time. Live here: have work to do. This for visitor." (He smiled disarmingly and indicated the assembly.) "For tourist."

I fled, blushing, mortified—and elated beyond words.

Olgivanna in the morning. I had just finished dressing and was standing by the window to recover from my exertions. My spirits rose at the sight of her, so fresh and lovely.

"I was on my way to the garden," she said. "But it is such an unseasonably warm day. I thought you might like to go for a walk."

"I am so glad you have come. There is nothing I would like better!"

We descended together and went into the garden. After we had walked a little way, I was obliged to sit and get my breath back. But I felt remarkably well.

"Really, Olgivanna, I am having a 'good day.' You know, I used to tell myself that good days—if they were days on which I had been unable to write—were not so very important since they did not necessarily add up to a good life, a life that can boast of some accomplishment. I thought that bad days were more likely to add up to something of lasting value, so long as I had written, and that is how I reconciled myself to them. But now I am not so sure: on this beautiful day I think it's important to have one's good days too. Perhaps it is because my work has changed. The work I am to do here is an inner work, a work on myself. That is not what my writing has been; but in future it will be different. But after all, do we not serve some higher purpose by being happy just as well as when we suffer? And what use is a work that does not give happiness?"

"The very happiness you feel today is the proof that you are doing a work that is right for you."

The note of conviction in her voice aroused my misgivings, which were never far away.

"Oh! do you think so? Because there is something I wish to ask you."

I put my hands on my knees and sat staring at the ground. I could feel my breath moving evenly and without difficulty, the cool air flowing in and out of my lungs, arousing no trace of irritation, no impulse to cough. The sun was warm on my hands and face, and all in all I felt like a healthy person—so long as I sat there quietly and did not exert myself. Wasn't this enough? What if life could be a succession of such moments?

"Yes, Katherine?"

"I do feel happy today," I asserted. "And entitled to my happiness! In the past I have always grasped at my happiness, as though it would be taken away if I did not possess it utterly. And of course it was taken away. Before I came here I felt that I had been separated from everything that I counted as my happiness: my husband, my writing, my dream of a home and a child. Then I came to see that my happiness was dependent upon me rather than upon the objects of my desire. But still, I thought, It is all to be denied me, the life that I wish to live."

I raised my head and looked across the lawn to the trees.

"Today I feel that life is mine!" I said, turning to Olgivanna. "Here and in this moment. And nothing else matters—for this moment. But what I wish to ask you is—the hope that seems to hover before me: Can I trust it? Can I reach out and touch it? Can I build up a life within me which death will not destroy?"

Olgivanna held my eyes with almost passionate intensity. She seemed to be looking into me, to divine what I could bear. But her expression betrayed no anxiety or sadness. At length, she put her hand on mine.

"There is no death for one like you who perceives the possibility of sweeping death aside when the time comes."

Here I began to cry. I closed my eyes and let the tears flow. Still I heard her voice, soft like a caress, yet ringing with conviction.

"I see that you have learned to value that which endures, the essence of life rather than 'living'—and this essence is your happiness! Your body is simply the medium through which you receive this thing that you love most. And if you learn how to keep it, how to separate what is permanent from the ephemeral, then you are no longer identified with your body. Disease, accident, death—or life: they do not concern you if you hold to the essential thing, which has become your happiness."

I bent my head down to my knees and continued to weep. I no longer felt any sense of constraint before Olgivanna: I was beyond all of that. She withdrew her hand and sat quietly by me until I was done. Then she took my hands and made me look at her.

"You feel it is true?" she said.

When I did not respond:

"What *do* you feel, Katherine?"

A sudden tremor—of joy! I lifted my head.

"I feel the sun's warmth," I said in wonder, "on my face and my hands."

FAITH

KM

Darling Bogey,

Suppose you were to throw up all your projects in England, resign your position, realize your capital—and come over here to work side by side with me. How do you like *that* for an idea? I would very much like for you to see the dancing. It would be useful for you, as a writer, it would give you a new outlook on art—and it simply cannot be described. Well, perhaps that is a rather slight reason for you to come. But there is far more than that here. It is not what you think, Jack, all smoke and mirrors; it is about getting free of the old mechanical life, in which we run from pillar to post, at the mercy of boils on the neck and a cold in the head and every bloody thought that passes through the mind. I am so sorry to hear you speak of your life as circumscribed by the four walls of your study and ridden by the demands of the paper. You know, it isn't just the physical constraints of such a life, it is the internal slavery, the living in a tiny little corner of oneself. Do you *like* such cramped quarters? Or are you burning somewhere deep inside to make a break for freedom? This, not rapping on the séance table, is the work here. Well, then, why not risk all—and throw in your lot with Wig—and with Gurdjieff?

You could help with the digging for the Turkish Bath and the building of the Study Hall. That sort of thing is really very much in your line, isn't it?—in spite of your book-wormishness. And if the worst came to the worst, if you really could not stand it, you could simply go away again, having assured yourself that I am in good hands. Throw it all up. What do you say? You have so many talents: you will always be able to support yourself in some way or other.

Perhaps this sounds like very wild talk to you. We are not very wild here, at all. Au contraire.

Ever your own
Wig

Strange and disturbing encounter with Jimmy Young. I was sitting outside on the terrace, within hailing distance of a work party, enjoying the colors of autumn, the intensely blue sky, the chilly air that makes distant objects stand out so sharp and clear. Patrick had insisted on going to the kitchen to fetch me a coffee. This he does on his own initiative; I do not like to disturb the cooks with trivial requests while they are preparing a meal for the entire community. Mr. Gurdjieff does it all the time, is Patrick's response. So I allow him to wait on me. The coffee that emerges is made the way Mr. Gurdjieff likes it, a scalding muddy brew. It will do you a world of good, Patrick claims. He is very solicitous, and I have quite lost my heart to him. A day on which I do not see him is a sad day for me.

Jimmy Young came out of the house and squatted down beside my chair. He lit a cigarette and without saying anything stared at the people working in the garden. I have come to feel comfortable in his presence and did not feel the need to say any-thing. But after a time he startled me by asking abruptly:

"What do you think of the people here?"

It happened to be a question to which I had given some thought. What *did* I think of the people here? How was my life with them different from the social life I had known?

"In one way," I said hesitantly, "they are no different from people everywhere, neither better nor worse. How should they be? But there is a special type of friendship here that I have not found anywhere else, that has very little to do with one's taste or affinity. There are people here that I cannot imagine associating with in any other circumstances. But I am united with them in trying to attain a common goal, and that makes all the difference. Or so it seems to me."

"I am afraid I must have missed that part of the experi-ence," Jimmy said. "What I find is that as time goes on I have less and less in common with the people here and I do not under-stand them at all."

This was more than simply a statement of fact. I sensed a grievance in his tone. For some reason, this made me uncomfortable, and I did not want to know about it, but before I could stop myself—

"Why is that?"

He tossed the cigarette away and turned to me eagerly, as if satisfied that he had secured an audience.

"Well, for one thing, their standard of culture falls far short of what Ouspensky led me to expect. They are persons of every sort, from an individual who claims to have been an officer of the Czar's bodyguard to a Paris taxi driver who looks like a *clochard*. Then there is the harem of young women who have been following Gurdjieff about for years. One cannot imagine what they think they are on to: for me they are the epitome of the so-called mechanical life that the Master always describes so scathingly. Apart from yourself and Orage and a few of the English, there isn't a soul with whom one can have an intelligent conversation, especially on the subject of what the devil is going on here. I had hoped to have something in common with our two doctors. But they seem to have abandoned their scientific curiosity upon passing the gate. The older one, the Russian, has an expression I can only liken to that of a solemn goat. It's not very easy to associate the idea of becoming more conscious with *him*. The younger one, the gentle giant, looks sagacious enough, but since he never says anything, it's impossible to tell."

All of this produced an unpleasant impression upon me. Was it because it echoed certain criticisms of people that I had entertained myself? At any rate, I wanted to put a stop to it, but I did not know how to do so without giving offense.

"And Gurdjieff has them all hypnotized!" he burst out again. "There is no other word for it. How else to account for the conviction, held by almost everybody around here, that Gurdjieff can do no wrong, that his every word and deed are divinely inspired, that he can see through one and know infallibly what one needs to do in each and every circumstance?"

I felt that my continued silence must surely be construed as agreement.

"I must confess that I worried about being hypnotized at first," I said. "But I find no evidence of it in my own dealings with

Mr. Gurdjieff. Sometimes I wonder if we make up his wonderful understanding. But one is always getting a fresh example of it..."

"Bah!" Jimmy said, almost rudely, "take this new car he has bought for himself. He has never driven a car before, much less owned one, yet everybody here is convinced that he does not need to learn. What about those ghastly noises when he attempts to put the thing in gear? He will end by killing himself and his passengers, if he does not destroy the gear box first. But try telling that to the faithful."

It was true that there was something terribly incongruous about Mr. Gurdjieff's appearance in the car, a sleek and massive Citroën. But I had the impression that he was as happy with it as a child with a new toy, and something in me admired him for his ability to revel in such impish happiness.

"This is what happens," Jimmy said, "when a man has been invested with the attributes of the all-powerful father, or when he has had the magician archetype projected onto him, as Jung would say. The people here are equally oblivious to criticism or common sense because they have projected their own unconscious power fantasies onto Gurdjieff. Of course, this does not happen by accident. He has invited it, he has created the conditions under which it can occur, so that in their eyes he can do no wrong. He is infallible. His every act has a hidden and wonderful significance. What he does is never to be taken at face value."

I felt that he had actually described what I had witnessed myself. And yet I rebelled against his characterization of Gurdjieff. I felt sure that it was not the only possible explanation of Gurdjieff's relations with his students. But for the moment I could think of nothing to say in Gurdjieff's defense.

"So you believe that Gurdjieff is not what he claims to be?" I said.

"What *does* he claim to be? Nobody seems to know. I believe he is first and foremost a megalomaniac. Didn't you notice the way he behaved toward the Russian couple in the wood the other day? What did you think of that little incident?"

"I thought it was contrived in order to teach us about different kinds of pride. You don't think so?"

Jimmy smiled mirthlessly and shot me a pitying glance.

"It was a tremendously instructive incident," he allowed. "But as for contrived—why, the man is as proud as a peacock! He is as touchy as can be, and he cannot stand the thought that people are talking about him behind his back. That is why he strives so hard to make a virtue of his pride. But his play-acting is for real. Why do people not see this? If it looks like pride and conceit, then damn it all, the chances are that it *is* pride and conceit!"

His voice quivered in exasperation. I supposed that he had spoken like this to a number of people and found no one who shared his point of view. I did not feel sympathetic to him myself— partly on account of his unpleasant manner, which I had never seen before in him—but I could not help remembering how convincing Gurdjieff's play-acting had been.

"There is no doubt that Gurdjieff is a personality to be reckoned with," Jimmy went on when I did not say anything, "no doubt at all about his many talents. I must admit that I've never met anyone quite like him: it is an extraordinary event in the life of a psychologist, and I intend to deliver a paper on the subject to my colleagues in the Society as soon as I get back to London. I begin to see that the time of my departure is rapidly approaching."

"Oh, dear," I said involuntarily.

I knew that I would be sorry to see him go. I felt warmly toward him, in spite of the agitation that his impressions of Gurdjieff and the others at the Prieuré had aroused in me. He had been helpful and considerate in numerous ways, and I had admired his matter-of-fact approach to the life and work here.

He leaned toward me confidentially.

"To tell you the truth, my dear, I have become persona non grata. It is dangerous to voice any criticism of the Master. I have been told that I suffer from spiritual pride, that I have not really accepted the conditions here, that I haven't worked on myself in the true sense. Well! Is one supposed to leave one's critical faculties behind when one enters the place? I don't wish to make a nuisance of myself, and so I am going away. But I have had an adventure, and I am well content."

"You are not disappointed then?"

"On the contrary!" he exclaimed, getting to his feet and vigorously thrusting his hands into his pockets. He began to stamp back and forth in front of my chair. "I came because I felt myself getting a little stale in my work with my patients and in my personal life. I am particularly interested in the question of will, and it seemed to me from my first acquaintance with the system that Gurdjieff offered a new approach to this question. How is one to unify the will? But it turns out to be something that is really not so new. Essentially, the problem of will does not arise here, since we are all of us required to submit to Gurdjieff's will or to surreptitiously evade it, which is what a great number of people are doing. Since one cannot control oneself, one submits to the control of another. No doubt there is something to be gained from this externally imposed discipline: one acquires the willingness to obey, the readiness to face difficulty, and perhaps a number of salutary mental and physical habits for good measure. But remove the external directives, and the problem of individual will presents itself once more. I doubt that the people who have been with Gurdjieff longest—the Russians and the gaggle of young women—would even be able to feed themselves if he were suddenly to leave them in the lurch."

It was with some relief that I saw Orage come around the corner of the house. He walked slowly, carrying something in his hand. Jimmy had his back to him and did not notice.

"Surely Gurdjieff is aware of this," he said. "Then what is he up to? I must admit that his intentions still elude me. He is a person who seems to thrive on mystery—or mystification. But this much I am sure of: the whole business is a personal enterprise, which he undertakes for his own benefit. There is a path to God and a path to Power. Ask yourself which path we find here. Ask yourself about the implications of the methods employed, the public humiliations, the confrontations. Even if such methods were to succeed in producing will, it would be merely a will to Power, and the advance of the soul toward God would be nil. One arrives at the wedding feast without the essential wedding garment. Love, compassion, spirituality: surely these are conspicuous by their absence here. I am ready to believe that a sufficiently lengthy acquaintance with Gurdjieff might result in the possession of certain powers, but I believe that one would remain under his control, constrained to use such powers for *his* personal ends, whatever they might be. They have nothing to do with God and the desire for God, of that I am sure. In fact, it seems to me that there are signs of hoofs and horns all over this place—"

Orage stepped forward and handed me a cup of steaming coffee.

"Compliments of Patrick, who has been called on the carpet about something or other. Can I have a word with you, Jimmy?"

They walked off together in the direction of the work party, Orage with his hand resting lightly between Jimmy's shoulder blades, leaning toward him and talking to him seriously and quietly. Jimmy halted abruptly, and a more animated conversation ensued, just out of the range of my hearing. I felt sure that they were having an argument and that it had something to do with me. Finally Jimmy turned on his heel and walked away swiftly in the direction of the forest. Orage came back to me, drew a chair near to mine, and sat for a while without saying anything.

"I appreciate the way I have been taken care of here," I said at length. "People have been extraordinarily considerate of my condition. But is it really necessary to protect me from every word of dissent?"

Orage shot me a look of surprise. Then he bowed his head, as if acknowledging that I had guessed his intention. I was touched.

"Am I not capable of making up my own mind?" I teased him.

He smiled back, and we exchanged a look of understanding. It was not necessary for him to say that he knew Gurdjieff to be my last hope, that he feared for me if I were to be deprived of it.

"I am not so easily turned aside when I have taken a decision," I told him, "especially one that has cost me as much as my decision to come here."

"Yes, yes," he murmured, ceasing to smile and looking into my face.

"I don't claim to know all the influences that brought me to it," I said, "nor what Gurdjieff is up to, as Jimmy Young puts it. But I am content not to know, or to know how little I know. I know that this is the place for me. If I were anywhere else, I would be completely at a loss."

"I am glad to hear it," Orage said.

"But it was an uncomfortable conversation, and I'm glad you interrupted it."

Orage sighed and stared off across the lawn toward where Jimmy had disappeared.

"I'm afraid Jimmy has painted himself into a corner," he said. "He has come to a particularly sticky place in his own work. There is something that he has to see, about himself, but he persists in looking only at the people around him and at their relations with Mr. Gurdjieff. He wants to analyze things in accordance with his own ideas, whereas what he needs is to observe himself, in order to have material for analysis. I made the mistake of pointing this out to him, and as a result I have joined the ranks of those who are not sympathetic. It is a great pity. I have known him for many years, and I am very fond of him."

"Is there nothing one can do?"

Orage sank deeper in his chair and stretched out his legs. I was touched by the frank expression of his affection for Jimmy Young. When I knew him in London, he had always been meticulously courteous, but at the same time, reserved. Here he seemed physically exhausted—and marvelously at ease.

"That is the trouble with this work," he said "It can separate people."

He gave me a quick look from under his brows, as if to gauge a reaction.

"Or perhaps I should say that the Work makes it possible for people to come together in a new way. But we cannot bring others to it; we can only work on ourselves."

"Mr. Orage!"

Patrick's head protruding from a second floor window.

"Mr. Orage! Mr. Gurdjieff would like to see you in his room!"

Orage got to his feet with a sigh.

"I hope I haven't been tiring you, my dear," he said. "Can I help you inside?"

"Thank you, no. I believe I will sit here and think about what you have said."

He hastened away. I had the impression that he would rather have sat and talked with me than faced a summons to Gurdjieff's room. I was left alone with the melancholy effect of his words: We cannot bring others to this work. I thought of Jack and me. How difficult it is to accept that my desire to be here has separated us! Are we swiftly and silently moving away from each other, as Jack writes? I want to say, No! a thousand times no! Whatever is taking place between us, it is, it *must* be for the good. But can we help each other, as of old? What of the communion of work? Can we ever *work* together again?

2 XI 22
Le Prieuré

My own Bogey,

I am so ashamed of my last letter. Its tone is all wrong—and yet it is so like me. When I discover something that is new, it is fearfully hard for me not to be intense, and when I am intense, I am always a little bit false. Now I will have to go back to the beginning and start again. I have worked so little and understand so little; it is so wrong for me to tell you what you should think or feel about something that I have scarcely begun to explore myself. Perhaps you can have dinner with Ouspensky the next time you are in London. He can tell you about the ideas so much better than I can. It is folly for me to even mention them—that is why I write so little.

Not so very much happens here, Boge, at least to all appearances. It is true that life here is quite different from anything I have ever known, but violent changes to one's individuality—of course, they do not occur. Underneath the surface, a great deal takes place, but it is not the sort of thing that can be described, not by the likes of your Wig who cannot even write a sensible letter any more, not while the struggle takes place between the old self and the new. I must not even mention this struggle because it can mean nothing to one who is not engaged in it—and it is presumptuous of me to think that I *can* engage in it: I am merely nibbling at it, I am putting my toe in the water, nothing more.

And I must not fly off at tangents and suggest, however frivolously, that you should turn your life upside down in order to join me here. I did not mean it, Boge. Forgive me. Coming here is a very serious step. It was wrong of me to suggest that you should come here for any other reason than a sincere desire to obtain what this place can give—for yourself. I believe it is the place for *me*. I know I shall never grow strong anywhere in the world except here.

As for you and I, let's be honest: what present relationship have we? None. But I feel that we are nonetheless together, that we belong to each other. Oh, my dearest, just wait and see how you and I will live and love one day—so happily, so splendidly...

3 November

It comes again at night while I am lying abed, like a vision, like a waking dream, in the most startling immediacy, as though I am constrained to walk through the events of the past, just as they were, nay, more so, for there is lacking the excitement I felt, the hectic sense of anticipation and uncertainty about how things would turn out—that is gone, for now all is known, and there is only the sadness of the observer who knows that all is fated, who is constrained to witness events without the protective veil of subjectivity, to see no longer through a glass darkly, but in a strange neutral light. There is no sense of volition, no possible chance to cut it off and turn away before it is done...

Therefore: Saturday, 4 July, 1909, on board the S.S. *Maori*, for Lyttelton. The Ladies Cabin: Mother and I sitting together in a strangled silence. The curtained portholes, the dim lights, the steward going into the smoking room with a tray, stepping over the high brass-faced step: I see it all, I am *there*, plunged in an agony of excitement, apprehension, and impatience to get away—from my family, from New Zealand, from everything. My ship, the *Papanui*, is to leave on Monday from Christchurch, but that seems like an eternity to spend in close quarters with my parents. I am sailing to the other side of the world: could they not have let me travel to the South Island unaccompanied? But Father asserted that I could not very well go down there alone...

Father puts his head in, ruddy-faced, brisk.

"Would one of you care for a walk before you turn in? It's glorious up on deck."

I rise at once. Mother is tired and irritable, and I am only too glad to get away from her. Father holds the door for me, leaning across it while I step out. I precede him on the companionway, breathing the sea air that wafts down from above. The brass stair-rail, the rubber stairs, a whiff of wayward exhaust from the funnels. Then: the deck. The frozen look of the ship by moonlight, the most functional objects, lifeboats and ventilators and stays, all charged with ghostly significance. And underlying all, the deep hum of the engines, steadying and reassuring even when unnoticed.

I walk swiftly to the rail. There is an absorbed pause while Father lights his cigar. Then he joins me, puffing contentedly. The sea below us is like a sheet of frosted glass—and far far below its surface, the turmoil of my feelings.

"There is something I want to tell you, Kathleen."

I recognize the tone, and something closes up inside me. I am obliged to listen, but I withdraw from him even as I stand there looking out. I am buried within myself, miles deep. I have grown a thick impervious skin that his grossness cannot penetrate.

"You have caused your mother and me some distress lately, as you well know. It is somewhat against my better judgment that I have given my blessing to your leaving us. I find at the last that I cannot stand in your way, but I want you to remember that it is an unusual concession we are making, one that many families wouldn't even consider."

His voice and manner are more suited to his trite and unfunny stories; there is something pathetic about his attempt at seriousness. It makes me squirm inwardly, with something very like shame—for him!—in spite of my effort to keep it at bay.

"When you go aboard the *Papanui*, and when you arrive in London, you will be a representative of this family. I want you to be aware of this—and to comport yourself accordingly."

One more day. Once out of sight of land a great weight will be lifted from me. Nothing but the sea, shining like the surface of another planet. If I never come to London at all, I will be content—just to be free of "this family."

"Do you hear me now, Kathleen?"

"Yes, Father," I muse distantly, without turning my head.

A sharp exhalation.

"Damn it all, I will not have you fooling around in dark corners with fellows—or with anyone! I'm telling you now for the last time. Do you know that your mother is worn away to a shade with worry about you?"

I turn slowly to meet his eyes. He looks away. He cannot look at me. I am torn between my disgust and the obligation of gratitude he has placed me under. But I cannot stand it any longer, not even "for the last time."

I place my hand apologetically on his sleeve.

"I am tired, Father."

I turn and walk away, still seeing him standing at the rail, his aggrieved and baffled eyes, his long drooping red-gray mustache, the cigar poised in his upraised hand.

Sunday in Christchurch. Sitting with Mother in the hotel. If my eyes follow a woman through the lobby, she will make some inane remark to distract me. I know that if I go up to the room, she will find an excuse to follow me. My impatience to be gone is like a fever, to be free from her suspicions, from her constant overbearing tyranny!

Monday at last, dark and pouring with rain. I pretend to sleep for as long as I can. Lunch in apathetic silence; even my parents' prodigious capacity for small talk is exhausted. Through the tunnel to the harbor in the foul-smelling gaslit train.

The unctuous Captain Weston, with whom Father's importance demands an audience, in his stateroom.

"Well, Beauchamp, letting this one leave the family nest, are you?"

"We have family over there, as you know, Tom. She won't be going among strangers."

The steward hands my father a whiskey, my mother a cup of tea. I have refused refreshment and sit silent in my churlishness. They continue to talk of me as though I were a suitcase that must not be misplaced.

"Of course we would rather she remain at home, Captain Weston," my mother informs him punctiliously. "But nothing will do her but to return to London."

"Aha," the captain pronounces mincingly. "Wellington is no longer good enough for her."

"She's literary," my father says. "She's hoping to have a brilliant career in England."

"London is the place for her then. She'll find plenty of literary people there. Maybe she'll have her fill of them before she's done."

This is a trifle too familiar for Mother.

"We have family there, Captain Weston" she reminds him. "I trust that she'll be in good hands aboard ship."

"In the very best of hands," Father assures her before the captain can speak up. "Tom is more than just an admirable sailor. He knows how to look after his passengers."

"Are there many women traveling?" Mother wants to know.

"Not many women on this trip, I'm afraid. Two or three, traveling with their families."

My mother's face is a mask of propriety.

"But we'll look after her, Mrs. Beauchamp. Never fear. If she were to take an interest in the ship now, I could make the voyage pass in a thrice for her, I assure you. Maybe she'll put it in a book someday—and make us all famous. Eh, Ms. Beauchamp?"

Tiresome old hypocrite!

Oh, the rain! drumming on the decks, the lifeboats, pocking the oily surface of the water. But Father and Mother insist on standing together on the wharf beneath a single umbrella, and this obliges me to remain on deck in the partial shelter of a ventilator, facing them across a gulf of rain-filled gloom, too far to hear what they are saying to each other or to discern their expressions, issuing an occasional desultory wave.

At last, at long long last, the unloosing of the cables, the sudden tremor of movement, the slow heart-stopping glide of the great bulk of the ship past the wharf. Two figures recede, waving. I wave too, though there are no lights near me and I feel sure they can no longer see me. Then, with a little start of surprise, as though I am not quite ready, I see them turn and walk away together, still huddling under the umbrella. Two or three steps in the rain and the gathering dusk and they have disappeared from view...

This recurrence of past events—it is quite a common thing with me nowadays since my sleep has been disrupted. It no longer seems strange to me that one can live again in the past, that the past should exceed the present in its immediacy. But there was something different about this particular visitation. My consciousness, my point of view, seemed diffused among the actors: I was no longer simply Kass, my father's most original and obstreperous child, who had by dint of alternating pleas and protests won his grudging permission to leave the family and begin her life's journey alone and unaccompanied. The fog of my own subjective impressions—my impatience, my disgust—seemed to be dispelled while I watched, and I felt rather than saw what my parents' experience had been. Thus I was a part of Mother's boredom, her anxiety on my behalf, her irritation at being dragged down to Christchurch—for she did not really want to go—her exhaustion, her envy at the prospect that lay before me, for *she* had not escaped, she was obliged to bend her neck to the yoke of family, to retrace her steps, to remain behind. And Father's disappointment as I left him standing at the rail, the flash of irritation that subsided into a brief sentimental melancholy: I am parting with the first of my children and this is how she treats me. I remembered—remarkably without rancor or guilt—all the various ways in which I am indebted to him, for a London education, an allowance of one hundred pounds a year, the entire world of my New Zealand stories, if the truth be told. And I remembered all of my many complaints against him that I had voiced to Olgivanna, this accompanied by a clear piercing remorse that lasted perhaps thirty seconds, hardly more, yet as long as I could bear. Not that those complaints are unjustified. But simply this: no complaint is justified when it is directed against the gift of life. If it weren't for my father, for the family I come from, I should lack that which is of most value in me, my desire to render my experience faithfully in writing, my desire for the truth. When one knows this—as I did in my thirty seconds of remorse—when one sees both sides, when one realizes the interdependence of all things, one gives up complaint: it simply becomes irrelevant. But to know it, to feel it, to enter into it, to the depths of one's being...

My father's parting present, the little brass pig that used to belong to my grandma, that I admired and he had given me, that will be returned to him when my will is executed...

5 November

Patrick wants me to see his chickens. I am so unabashedly happy that he has remembered me! I take this invitation to mean that he is not avoiding me.

The chicken pen is in a small shady yard at the back of the house. The fences look solid; in some places there are two layers of wire. We enter through a small wooden gate that Patrick is careful to secure behind us. The coops are lined against the wall of the house on one side of the enclosure, opposite a long low trough with water. Chickens are not fastidious creatures. There is a strong smell, and the ground underfoot is spattered their mess. But Patrick is making a valiant effort to keep all shipshape. The earth has been recently raked and swept, and there are piles of straw and leaves against the fence beside a neat row of garden tools, a shovel, rake, and pitchfork.

Our arrival has stirred up a great deal of activity. The chickens, brown and black and white, with startling red crests, bustle about us, some of them pecking at my feet.

"Perhaps they are hungry," I say. "Can I feed them something?"

"Chickens are always hungry," Patrick says.

He walks over to a bin beside the coop, lifts the lid and dips his hand in, then thrusts his hand in his pocket. He shoos away the chickens gathered about his feet and comes back to me, grinning.

"Here's some corn," he says conspiratorially, reaching in his pocket and swiftly pouring some into my palm. "Mind they don't peck your hand. You have to broadcast it."

"Thank you, Patrick," I say, emulating his seriousness. "This is a new experience for me. We had chickens when I was a little girl. And an Irishman—whose name was Pat!—to look after them. But he did not allow the children to feed them."

Patrick looks gratified.

"That is because chickens are wild when it comes to feeding," he says knowledgeably.

As if to confirm his description, they come surging around me as soon as I expose the corn in my hand. I scatter some grains, and they rush about trying to find them, jerking to and fro and pecking at each other in their agitation.

"Oh, how wonderful! I feel so terribly important."

Patrick, watching, frowns, one hand on his hip, the other atop the crown of his head, holding his lank hair out of his eyes.

"Will you please get me one? I want to pet it."

He corners a large white hen between the coops and the house and emerges after a brief scuffle with it in his arms.

"Hold her tightly," he instructs me. "She won't break."

Holding the hen, absorbing its warmth through the feath-ers, watching the nervous darting of her narrow head, for a mo-ment I feel connected to the earth and its creatures, to that part of my childhood when I lived in my senses. The dirt of the chicken yard about my feet, the cool air of November upon my face and neck, Patrick squinting against the weak sunlight, indecipherable voices from within: there is nothing else.

I bend over, and the hen leaps from my arms and scuttles away to join the rest of them.

"What is that one called, Patrick?"

He glances after it, shrugs.

"There are too many of them. I can't keep up with them anymore."

Hands thrust in his pockets, he moves away toward the gate.

"And anyway," he remarks, "Mr. Gurdjieff says that chick-ens are not very important, that they are very stupid."

"I suppose they are," I say, a little alarmed by his sudden petulance. "But I thought you liked them."

"Eggs for the breakfast, meat for the dinner," he recites. "That's all they're good for."

We pass out of the pen. Patrick bends over to fasten the gate. He is a long time about it, as though he doesn't wish to look at me. Then he straightens up abruptly, and I catch sight of tears upon his cheeks. He walks out into a little clearing beyond the house. I follow him warily. He seems to remember that I cannot walk very quickly and comes back to me. I sit on a tree trunk, and he stands beside me, his arms crossed upon his chest, staring off into the forest.

"When I was a little girl," I venture, "our gardener Pat made me watch him kill a chicken. And I was very upset. But after a little while I got over it, and I didn't feel so bad anymore."

"How did he kill it?" Patrick comes out with.

"Why, I don't think you would like to know."

"Did he chop off its head with an sword?" he persists.

"With an axe, Patrick. How did you know?"

"That's the way my grandfather used to do it," he says scornfully. "It's the way everybody does it. Except for Miss Madi-son. Did the chicken run away after he cut its head off?"

"Yes, Patrick. It gave me such a fright. I wanted Pat to put its head back on again. Wasn't that foolish of me?"

"Do you know why it runs away like that?"

"Please tell me, Patrick."

"It's because its feet don't know that its head is gone. That's what my grandfather said."

"That is a good explanation. Pat the gardener gave me a hug and told me not to cry. He was a good man. He took very good care of the chickens, when all was said, just as you do."

Patrick turns his face away from me with a sudden jerk.

"Miss Madison is not a good woman," he recites in an odd monotone. "She is not my friend."

"Oh, dear."

"I hate her! I hate her!" he gasps, in two little choked-off coughs.

The tears begin to trickle down his partially averted face. He is holding himself tightly, as though to suppress his feeling. His impotent rage touches me very deeply. My heart feels sore in my chest. But I cannot put my arms around him as I wish to, for fear that he will take fright and run away.

I hold out my handkerchief to him.

"Here, Patrick."

He opens his eyes for an instant and shuts them again. Fearfully, I reach out and take his hand. His body gives a little jump, and then to my surprise he squeezes my hand tightly in his and begins to cry unrestrainedly. He is almost hurting me, but I am determined to bear it and not to withdraw my hand. Shortly enough he is done. He gently releases my numbed fingers and walks away a few paces to stand with his back to me.

"Perhaps we can have a word with Mr. Gurdjieff," I venture.

"It's no use talking to him," Patrick bursts out tearfully. "I already know what he will say. Must bear unpleasant manifestations of others. That's all he *ever* says."

I sit there with the shadows of leaves moving upon my arms, feeling my incapacity. This poor child is an orphan, without any one to give him the care and love that he needs. But surely I can do something, even if I am only a passing stranger.

He sits down abruptly on the ground, still with his back to me.

"I'm sorry you're unhappy, Patrick. You are a good boy. Is there anything you would like?"

"I would like to go to my own room," he retorts. "But I can't."

"Why not?"

"Mr. Gurdjieff says I must not leave you alone if no one else is near."

My eyes fill with tears, and a lump rises in my throat. It is a couple of minutes before I am able to speak.

"You are taking very good care of me, Patrick," I say carefully. "Perhaps we can take care of each other. Why don't you come and sit beside me on the tree? We will sit here without saying anything and maybe the answer will come to us, out of the air."

After a moment's hesitation, he comes and sits beside me. I pass him the handkerchief and he wipes his face. As we sit there without speaking, I become aware of the sound of the wind. What an interesting sound it is when one attends to it, how rich and complex, how evocative of the most subtle shades of feeling that are normally imperceptible. And it occurs to me that the whole of our experience is like that, infinitely rich and varied, but we do not notice it, immersed as we are in the turmoil of our feelings and our thoughts.

And of course as soon as I have begun thinking in this manner, I am no longer aware of the wind and what it evokes. Instead there is the strange heart-sickness of my longing to comfort Patrick, a certain lightheadedness—and a sense of utter exhaustion. How will I ever get back to my room?

A sigh from Patrick recalls me to the moment. Should I ask him if he feels better? Or would it be preferable to ignore his distress and change the subject?

While I am considering:

"Where did you live when you were my age, Mrs. Murry?"

"What age *are* you, Patrick?"

"I'll be ten in January."

"Goodness. I thought you were at least eleven. You are very grown up."

"That is what everybody says," Patrick informs me proudly.

"When I was ten years old I lived in New Zealand, which is very far away from here, eleven thousand five hundred miles, to be exact."

"Do you miss it?"

"Very much. I have lived in England for a long time now, but it is not *my* country."

A sudden painful longing for New Zealand comes over me. Patrick seems to be the catalyst for such experiences. I don't want England. It is of no use to me, in my work, in my life; it will never be of use to me.

"England is *my* country," Patrick says. "But my father lives in America. I do not miss England. I want to be here with Mr. Gurdjieff. He is very like my grandfather."

"How is that, Patrick?"

"Everybody is afraid of him."

"Were people afraid of your grandfather, Patrick?"

He shrugs.

"Were *you* afraid of him?"

"He didn't yell at *me*. But he yelled at my mother when she said that she wouldn't look after his dog, Old Malachy."

"Oh, dear."

Patrick's forehead crinkles into an exquisite little frown.

"It was after my father went away to America. Old Malachy was sick. My mother had him put to sleep. Then my grandfather died. I do not tell him about Old Malachy when I talk to him. He would be very angry with my mother."

I am not a fit companion for a child. I do not know what to say when it is time for me to demonstrate the adult's equanimity.

"My mother had to take Old Malachy to the vet. She didn't want me to come with her, but she couldn't get Old Malachy to go in the office without me. He was shaking all over when the vet put him on the table. I held on to him and the vet gave him the injection and he lay down very quick and closed his eyes. He's sleeping, the vet said. But I knew he wasn't. I ran out and banged my forehead against the door and got a lump on it. My mother said we could have another dog, but we never did. She sent me to my aunt and went back in the hospital."

I sit there helplessly, fretting for him, but unable to find words of comfort.

"But now I *have* another dog," Patrick says, becoming suddenly animated. "Mr. Gurdjieff's dog, Philos. I am supposed to look after Philos, to make sure he has enough to eat and drink. I am the only person he will let come in the room if Mr. Gurdjieff is not there."

"I'm sure your grandfather would be happy to know that you have found another dog."

He turns to me with a puzzled expression. I look back at him, waiting for something to come to me, out of the air.

"Do you remember what you asked me the other day, Patrick? You wanted to know if the people we love continue to live after they die. When I lived in New Zealand, I had a grandma that I loved very much. Then I went away to England, and when I came back she died before I could go to see her. If you continue to love your grandfather, he will continue to live—for you. My grandmother is still alive for me; she is very close, since I have been here. I feel that she is looking after me, like a guardian angel. And I am sure that your grandfather is doing the same for you."

"Do you talk to her?" Patrick asks conscientiously.

I am about to say that it isn't possible to talk to someone who has passed away. But something gives me pause. I was going to say this because I thought that Patrick needed to hear it, because I thought it would be wrong of me to encourage a belief in the supernatural in a young child. But I myself did not know what I believed; in fact, I had come to a point at which belief was irrelevant. When I thought about such things I became confused and frightened, and yet when I felt my grandmother's benign presence—as I have on many a recent sleepless night—I experienced no confusion or fright: it seemed a perfectly natural thing. Why then should I speak to Patrick out of received opinion?

"I shall try, Patrick. And I will let you know what she says."

"She may not say anything for a long time," Patrick says knowingly. "But that doesn't mean she isn't listening."

"I will keep that in mind, Patrick," I say, wondering who is giving comfort to whom. "Now if you will walk with me back to my room..."

I get up and face about. Patrick takes my elbow lightly and supports it, as no doubt he has seen adults do. The expression on his face is one of grave concentration.

"What is America like, Mrs. Murry?" he asks when we have reached the top of the stairs.

"I've never been there, Patrick."

"I would like to go there some time."

I have to turn my head to conceal my tears.

"I'm sure you will, Patrick."

7 November

I had often been told that Mr. Gurdjieff likes to set the house "walking," to assign our people to different rooms, in order to upset their routine. For some reason, this phrase reminded me of a part of one of Chekhov's letters written en route to Sakhalin—about bed bugs, the scourge of Siberian accommodations: "When it's really cold," a Siberian peasant tells the traveler, "the bed bugs don't walk." Well, it is quite sufficiently cold at the Prieuré and there are no bed bugs to speak of, but the entire household has been set "walking," and there is no end of confusion and complaint.

I have a new room—and a new life. My old room was rich and sumptuous, in a wing of the Prieuré reserved largely for visiting dignitaries, called the Ritz by those who were not privileged to live there. It was sedate and quiet; you felt that you were in an affluent apartment building whose tenants kept discreetly to themselves. My new room is small and plain and very simple—and outside my door all is uproar and confusion! Comings and goings at all hours, voices through the walls, the corridor a major thoroughfare, and a creaky staircase with people dashing up and down. But I do not mind it in the least! It makes me feel that I am a part of the community here and no longer merely a tourist. Can this be the same Katherine who suffered so much for her privacy's sake in hotels and pensions throughout Europe? Answer: it is not the same Katherine. That Katherine is but sleeping—and could at any moment awake. But in the meantime, what joy! what freedom! I used to think when Lawrence talked of community that I could not bear it, the company of women in particular. But the women here are nearer and far dearer to me than the men—with the exception of Patrick.

Olgivanna helped me to move in. There is one great advantage to my new room: it is so small that the merest scrap of a fire suffices to heat the air to a tropical temperature. In fact, one strives to get away from the fire and has to open the door. After Olgivanna washed her yellow dancing stockings, she hung them from the mantelpiece to dry. We sat together on the bed—there is nowhere else to sit—and felt like two young girls, poor but filled with hope.

"Olgivanna," I said. "Why do Patrick's guardians visit him so infrequently?"

"Oh, it's a sad story. His aunt, on her own admission, is entirely unsuited to take the place of his mother. The very thought that he is dependent upon her makes her want to run away. Her companion—they are a couple, you know—alternates between strictness and laissez faire. It was her idea to leave Patrick at the Institute. She says that it is good for him to be on his own and to have responsibilities. But there seems to be no one who is willing to take responsibility for the poor child, except Mr. Gurdjieff."

"Does his aunt wish to be rid of him? Is that why she agrees to leave him here?"

Olgivanna gave me a quick questioning glance. Perhaps she had divined the direction of my thoughts.

"I feel sorry for him," I said, blushing and looking away.

"I cannot say what she wants. I do not know her. What I am telling you is merely gossip."

"But you have spoken with her."

"Oh yes," Olgivanna said. "About Mr. Gurdjieff and the Work. We have never spoken about Patrick."

I could tell from the sound of her voice that she was puzzled by me.

"Then perhaps you can introduce me," I said, bringing the conversation to a close. "She is a literary person. We will have something in common."

A week after I moved into my new room, a great clattering in the corridor, people running and shouting, "Vode! Vode!" ("Water!") I ignored it for as long as I could—my fire was out, but it was warm in bed—until at last I heard a familiar voice calling "Fire! Fire!" and there came a frantic pounding at my door. I sprang out of bed, quite forgetting myself in my alarm, threw on my fur coat, and opening my door beheld the blackened countenance of Patrick, his teeth bared and gleaming like a pirate's in the half-light of a candle that he held in his fist. The corridor was a press of people hurrying back and forth, bearing all sorts of receptacles, jugs, basins, buckets, chamber pots, bowls from the kitchen, even urns from the garden. "Vode! Vode!"

"Mrs. Murry! Mrs. Murry!" Patrick greeted me, as though I were standing at the far end of the room instead of right in front of him. "Rachmilevich has set his room on fire! The whole house may burn. You must go downstairs immediately!"

"Please close the door and let me get dressed."

Patrick cast a regretful glance at the corridor. He was obviously enjoying himself immensely. He closed the door and stood with his back to me and his ear to the door, attending to every nuance of the hubbub while I huddled into my clothes. For some reason I felt absolutely calm. At no point did I fear for my own safety or anyone else's. Yet I took the alarm seriously and dressed with unwonted efficiency.

"I told him it would happen!" Patrick exclaimed. "I told him!"

"Told who, Patrick?"

"I told Mr. Gurdjieff that Rachmilevich would set fire to his bed clothes. He smokes in bed. He even singed his beard and burned a hole in his shirt. I told Mr. Gurdjieff!"

Rachmilevich is one of those who escaped from Russia with Gurdjieff. Since the Russians keep to themselves and seldom take part in the activities of the Institute, I had never spoken to him. But I had noticed his dour countenance and his grating, querulous voice. He is one of those people for whom one feels an immediate, unreasoning dislike.

"And what did Mr. Gurdjieff say?"

"He said that he could not order Rachmilevich to stop smoking because Rachmilevich would not be able to obey him. You could tell him not to fall asleep with a lighted cigarette in his mouth! I said."

A crash from outside. Patrick flung the door open. Seizing the sleeve of my coat, he towed me out into the throng. Smoke eddied above our heads, and flames were visible at the far end of the corridor, beyond the stairs. Came the sound of heavy purposeful footsteps. People pressed back against the walls: Mr. Gurdjieff with a sledge hammer. Candlelight caught his shining pate and eyes as he rushed by. A moment later I saw the sledge hammer rise and fall with a decisive swing, and the floor shook as plaster and part of the ceiling came crashing down.

With many an anguished backward look Patrick ushered me down the stairs. When we reached the ground floor, where both of the great doors stood open to the night air, I dropped upon a chair, pulling my coat around me. Patrick stood by, literally jumping up and down.

"You may go back upstairs to help, if you wish," I told him. "But please be careful. I will be all right here, unless the place comes crashing down about my ears."

He was gone in a flash, tearing up the stairs. I sat there, facing the door. The light from the tall elegant wall sconces threw the outline of the doorway upon the dark lawn; beyond it all was pitch black. The cold air nipped at my cheeks, and I drew up the collar of my coat.

Orage emerged from the direction of the kitchen, staggering under the weight of a great vat of water. When he saw me, he looked about for a place to set it down, but I waved him away.

"I'm quite all right," I said. "Attend to the fire!"

"It is like the burning of Moscow," he managed, as he started up the stairs.

I felt remarkably sanguine for having been routed out of bed in the middle of the night. Instead of weariness there flowed in my limbs a little charge of excitement, and I was eager for Patrick to return with news.

The commotion above me continued for a long time. I felt like the witness of a distant battle, too far removed to interpret its confused tumult. Finally I was so tired that I could not rouse myself to the effort of closing the doors, even though I had to clench my teeth to keep them from chattering.

Patrick flopped down beside my chair, looking thoroughly exhilarated.

"Two rooms completely burned out!" he gasped. "Mr. Gurdjieff knocked down a wall and stopped the fire from spreading. Otherwise the whole corridor would have gone up in smoke! The whole Prieuré!"

"How is Mr. Rachmilevich?"

"He didn't even get a burn," Patrick said disgustedly. "And he refused to apologize to Mr. Gurdjieff. He said the Prieuré is a fire trap, and we'll all be burned to death in our beds some night—and Mr. Gurdjieff will be held responsible!

"But where is he to go?"

"He is to have the empty room next to yours," Patrick said, clapping his hand to his head and assuming a solemn expression. "You must ask Mr. Gurdjieff to move you immediately."

"What on earth for?"

Patrick regarded me silently for a moment, as though wondering whether I could be trusted. What a pleasure it was to see the changing expressions of his animated face!

"You don't know Rachmilevich," he said at length. "He does nothing but complain. He will drive you mad with his complaining!"

"I don't think that is too likely," I said cheerfully. "I cannot understand a word he says."

"He will keep you awake all night!"

"That is impossible, Patrick, since I cannot sleep anyway."

I was positively giddy with exhaustion—and with the enjoyment of our strange encounter.

"He will set the room on fire again!" said Patrick, virtually beside himself. "I will have to come and rescue you!"

"It is a great comfort to know that you are looking after me, Patrick," I said. "But perhaps Rachmilevich will have learned his lesson."

Patrick got to his feet and looked around him swiftly and furtively. There were some stragglers on the stairs, but no one within hearing. He leaned toward me, speaking in a loud whisper.

"Mrs. Murry. Rachmilevich is the Devil! He doesn't like anything here: the food, the animals, the people. He especially *hates* the children."

I began to feel some concern.

"What do you mean, Patrick?"

"He is always trying to get us into trouble. We don't want to have anything to do with him, but he is always spying on us and bearing tales to Miss Madison. And he knows everything! He does not care what the adults do, but if a child climbs the wall and goes to Avon, or if a child takes food from the adults' table, Rachmilevich knows about it—and sooner or later Miss Madison will know about it too. He is an *informer*."

He pronounced the word with almost comic distaste. I reminded myself that he was only ten years old. His highly developed sense of responsibility made one forget his age.

"You must ask Mr. Gurdjieff to move you! Will I take you to him?"

"At this hour of the night?" I said, trying to smile in spite of my fatigue. "Will you please help me to go upstairs? I presume that it is safe for me to go back to bed."

10 November

A most distressing episode. I hardly feel capable of describing it. But I am in such distress about the treatment of Mr. Rachmilevich—and about the role Patrick has played in it—that I must try to relieve my feelings in the old way...

Mr. Gurdjieff has gone to Paris and is not expected to return for at least a week. In his absence, the atmosphere of the Prieuré is changed. It is not that people do not continue to work at the various projects and discharge the duties that have been assigned them. The house is as busy as ever, but there is a holiday air about it, an air of laxity and ease. Miss Madison is in charge and bustles about officiously. But it is merely the semblance of authority and fools no one. The Master is away, and he has taken with him the sense of urgency that spurs one to make unpalatable efforts, to work against sleep.

I feel sure that this affair of last night could not have taken place if Gurdjieff had been here. It began at 11 PM with an uproar in the corridor. I was sitting by the remnants of my fire when a most extraordinary cacophony of sounds struck up outside my door, as though at the beck of a conductor's baton. There was a sound of wailing and inconsolable weeping, a high-pitched squeaking as though some creature were being tortured, and voices calling out in long blood-curdling whoops. For myself I was not unduly concerned. In shattering the silence, the din had interrupted a gloomy train of thought and reminded me that I was not alone in the house—or in the universe. I knew at once that the children were involved. There are about a dozen children here, and they form a little society of their own, relatively unsupervised by the adults, apart from Miss Madison, who oversees their chores. I began to be a little annoyed when the noise persisted, not so much for myself but on behalf of the rest of the inhabitants of the floor who must surely have been awakened. And then I succeeded in deciphering what the voices were calling out: "Mr. Rachmilevich! The end is nigh!"

I went to the door and opened it quickly. I saw four or five of the children prancing outside Mr. Rachmilevich's door. They were wearing masks made out of cardboard that covered their eyes. Some of them were playing frantically upon combs wrapped in toilet paper—that was the "creature" I had heard being tortured—one of them was producing a eerie piercing whistle by blowing into the mouth of an empty milk bottle, and the rest were shaking various noise-producing objects—a bell, a tambourine, a spoon inside a tin mug—to contribute to the overall effect.

"Will you children please stop making noise and go to bed—immediately!"

Of course, it was impossible to make oneself heard. At that moment the door next to mine was flung open, and Mr. Rachmilevich emerged. He was barefoot, with a decrepit robe hastily thrown over a short grubby nightshirt, and his appearance was greeted by an ear-splitting cheer. He hesitated for a moment and turned to look at me. His face was terribly drawn, and there were deep bluish hollows beneath his anguished eyes. I felt an intense aversion. What was it about his misery that so repelled me? Standing there in the midst of the uproar I felt suddenly that my presence might be misunderstood, and I took a step toward him. But the cheering persisted, and without warning Mr. Rachmilevich uttered a scream of rage and lunged at the nearest child. The youngster evaded him, and Mr. Rachmilevich stumbled, knocking his shoulder against the wall. But before I could go to his assistance, he had regained his balance and was running recklessly down the corridor. He teetered from wall to wall unsteadily, the robe flapped about his thin bony ankles, and the children fled before him, howling with delight.

I turned back to reenter my room. As I closed the door, I saw a small figure emerge from the stairway, cross the corridor, and enter Mr. Rachmilevich's room. I stood still for a moment, my hand on the door knob. Then I opened the door again and walked along the wall to where Mr. Rachmilevich's door stood open. I was almost knocked over on the threshold by Patrick, who was emerging from the room. He stared at me, wild-eyed and breathless; he scarcely seemed to recognize me in his excitement. My eyes went to something he was clutching to his chest. Instantly he snatched his hand behind him, but not before I saw what he had in it: a set of grotesquely large and discolored false teeth.

"Patrick!" I exclaimed.

I put out my hand to detain him, but he had slipped by me. Before I could call again, he was at the stairway, and I heard the tattoo of his agitated footsteps descending.

The house was quiet again. I stood for a while at the scene of the crime, feeling implicated in it myself. Then I went in my room and shut the door. I was cold and trembling; the fire was in ashes. I extinguished the candle, got into bed, and draped my fur coat on top of the bed clothes. What was I to do? If Mr. Gurdjieff had been here, I felt sure that I could have approached him and placed the matter in his hands. But Mr. Gurdjieff was in Paris. I could not imagine myself bearing tales to Miss Madison, Patrick's sworn enemy. I shuddered at the thought of a late-night tête-à-tête with Mr. Rachmilevich in his room. I felt sorry for him, but there was something about him that brought out the worst in me, and I wished to have as little as possible to do with him.

At length his weary footsteps were audible in the corridor. As they passed my door, they were accompanied by a disgruntled muttering that rose and fell as though he were haranguing a silent companion. His door was closed. I felt that I was under a clear obligation to tell him what I had witnessed, but I continued to lie there beneath the mound of the covers. I was thoroughly ashamed of myself, but I finally assuaged my feelings by resolving that I would speak to Patrick in the morning. I had no confidence that he would listen to me. His excited manner had made me feel that he did not respect me, and now I must assume the role of authority figure, to tell him as a parent might how to behave himself. I would rather not. But I have no choice, other than to betray him.

And before sleep, the extraordinary thought: Here I am all wrought up about something that is quite mundane and trivial—just as I used to be in the days when I thought that I would live forever.

12 November

A disgraceful sequel played out at the breakfast table. I had gotten up early to bring my coffee cup to the kitchen, and I encountered Mr. Rachmilevich on the stairs. His face was sunken on account of the absence of his teeth, and his expression of smoldering impotent rage shamed me anew. He nodded dourly, but did not offer to speak to me.

Returning from the kitchen, I heard a commotion from the Russian dining room. I glanced in at the doorway in passing—and beheld an astonishing sight: Mr. Rachmilevich, scarlet in the face, breathless with rage and exertion, rushing about the seated company in pursuit of a group of laughing children. I stared rudely, unable to help myself. Patrick was among the fugitives, so convulsed with laughter that he could scarcely flee. Something about his blissfully abandoned features disturbed me; it was a side of him that I could not know. And I was afraid Mr. Rachmilevich would lay hands upon him and do him an injury.

But Mr. Rachmilevich was more likely to injure himself. He stumbled about, knocking against the tables, upsetting teacups, falling against his compatriots, swinging his fists wildly. The truly dreadful thing was that any of the other people could have intervened, to arrest the mad scampering of the children or to restrain Mr. Rachmilevich—or both. But they behaved like the audience of a cabaret; they ate and drank and talked among themselves and now and then cast an amused glance in the direction of the chase. Apparently Mr. Rachmilevich had not endeared himself to his fellow countrymen. But the spectacle was humiliating for everyone concerned. Would no one put a stop to it?

I stood frozen in the doorway, where no one paid the slightest attention to me. I was the one who was at fault. I might have stopped Patrick from taking the teeth; I should certainly have spoken to Mr. Rachmilevich. I watched Patrick, casting about for a way to extricate him from the fray. He and another boy about the same age leaned together, helpless with laughter, throwing their heads back to look up, exchanging incredulous glances, and collapsing upon each other again. I raised my eyes to the ceiling—and to my horror I found that a bubble of laughter was forming itself in my throat. Mr. Rachmilevich's teeth were in plain view of the entire company, suspended from the gas fixture directly above his head.

I swallowed my heartless mirth as best I could. For an awful moment I thought it would be necessary for me to point the teeth out to him, in order to put a stop to the row. I had a ludicrous image of myself raising a warning arm above the heads of the company, mutely denoting the imminent wrath of God. But I was spared the necessity of such a dramatic gesture when Mr. Rachmilevich, becoming aware perhaps that the children were glancing at something above his head, looked up and espied his teeth.

To the accompaniment of derisive cheering, he mounted the table unsteadily, trampling on plates and cutlery, tottering on his feet. He stood there for a long time, worrying the knot that held the teeth in place, pathetically exposed in his funereal black suit, the narrow trousers of which did not quite reach the tops of his socks, so that his bony shins were visible. Eventually someone took pity on him and handed him a knife. He descended with a certain cold and silent dignity, hunched over his place at the table, and replaced the teeth in his mouth. The children continued their taunting cheers, but somewhat listlessly, and to no effect. Mr. Rachmilevich sat there, chewing wolfishly on a piece of bread. The anger had burned itself out in his eyes, and in its place there was the harried and beaten look of a wounded animal.

I felt greatly abashed—as though I were personally responsible for his humiliation. Perhaps some of the others felt guilty too. At any rate, they began to rise and leave the table. The children quickly dispersed. I looked around for Patrick, but he had disappeared. I felt that he had given me the slip. But I did not know what I wanted to say to him. I became aware that people had noticed me standing in the doorway, and I went away quickly.

To find oneself under an obligation to such a person as Mr. Rachmilevich, who is nothing to me save a pathetic spectacle and a goad to my lower nature—it is maddening!

And Patrick! His behavior has served to make me aware of my unfitness for the role of parent. If I were responsible for him; I should have to concern myself about whether or not he is acquiring bad habits. Probably a real mother would put a good part of it down to high spirits. Children are unconsciously cruel, but they mean no harm. No, that is not quite right. He was been allowed to run wild, and there is no one here to provide a steadying hand—or to protect him from the likes of Mr. Rachmilevich!

I want to help him, but I do not know how to address him. Because it matters so much to me—oh! so very much. I *cannot* say anything to him that might deprive me of his company.

I do wish that Mr. Gurdjieff were here.

17 November: The Notebooks of the Law

Scene: the room with the piano where I waited on my arrival, a great fire reflected in the tall uncurtained windows, the whole house assembled, having received a solemn summons: Mr. Gurdjieff will mete out the punishments tonight. The Master enthroned to one side of the fire, his slippered feet resting on a sheepskin, very serious and dignified, the firelight gleaming on his shaved head. On his right hand Miss Madison, sitting on the floor, her hands demurely folded upon a small black notebook, head bowed. My chair has been stationed on the other side of the fire, and as I look across at her, I am struck once again by how singularly unprepossessing her appearance is, how devoid of sex, of any trace of personal charm, with her ancient dresses that hang upon her bony frame as upon a coat hanger, her pale frosty features, iron gray hair drawn tightly into a bun, restless eyes that reveal no awareness of the impression she makes, nothing save for a remembrance of her role.

Most of the company is seated on the floor, in attitudes of attentiveness rather than repose, close together as though for safety, for there is an atmosphere of tense expectancy in the room. I find myself, being seated above the other students, once again uncomfortably juxtaposed to Mr. Gurdjieff. Thankfully all eyes are focused on him and on Miss Madison.

He lifts his head slowly and turns it from side to side to survey us. His glance does not quite reach me; I notice that most people keep their eyes downcast, as though they do not want to meet his look. A latecomer enters and scurries into place. Mr. Gurdjieff waits for silence. His face is devoid of expression, so that before he speaks it is impossible to know what the tone of the meeting will be, save from the knot of anxiety in my own stomach and the extremely serious, not to say fearful, expressions of everyone else.

"Miss Madison," he intones at last in a rather theatrical voice, that of a slightly disreputable auctioneer opening the proceedings of an auction. "Please read the 'offenses.' Be so kind."

He imparts a special ironical inflection to "offenses" and looks about him again with a faint smile, as though to see if this is appreciated.

Miss Madison opens the notebook and begins to read in a stilted and monotonous voice that is somehow the perfect expression of her character. To my horror, Patrick's name heads the list.

"Patrick Miller—has left the grounds of the Prieuré without permission at every opportunity. Threw down and destroyed a garden statue of the Winged Victory of Samothrace because he claimed that it would frighten the younger children. Put the earth back in a hole that Mr. Orage dug for the kitchen plumbing so that Mr. Orage was obliged to dig it again. Repeatedly left Mrs. Murry's chair out in the rain overnight. Dug up and disposed of a delphinium plant in the flower garden. Failed to mend holes in chicken pen and to sweep the yard of chicken droppings. Neglected to perform gatekeeper duty on at least three occasions. Deliberately bent the tines of a dinner fork when told not to do so. Kept residents of the monks' corridor awake by making offensive noises and playing upon paper and comb. Entered Mr. Rachmilevich's room surreptitiously and without his permission, removed his teeth from the glass of water by his bedside—and suspended same from gas fixture in dining room!"

Miss Madison succeeds in giving a slight declamatory emphasis to the final offense and then ceases to read. The silence is deafening. I glance around for Patrick, but can not see him. Mr. Gurdjieff, who has allowed his head to fall forward on his chest as though bored by the recitation, now raises it again and looks around him.

"Patreek!"

"Here, Sir!" comes from Patrick in an absurdly prompt schoolboy squeak.

Mr. Gurdjieff waves his hand dismissively.

"Read."

There is a palpable easing of the tension, and Miss Madison resumes her reading. I do not listen very attentively to her litany of offenses. It seems to go on forever, and I have the impression that I am the only person in the room whose name is not mentioned; apparently Miss Madison's intelligence system has not enabled her to discover that I accepted some of her flowers that were cut by Olgivanna. There are some comic annotations, which Miss Madison delivers in a flawlessly business-like manner. Mr. Pinder, having smashed his thumb, has hurled the offending hammer into a pond from which it has not been retrieved. Olgivanna, upon hearing that she is assigned to take care of the newly acquired pigs, has expressed her feelings by means of an improper exclamation (not specified). Mr. Rachmilevich, receiving his comeuppance, is taken to task for the amount of crockery that has accumulated in his room.

Mr. Gurdjieff listens impassively, his head resting upon his hand in an affectation of weariness, occasionally glancing at one of the offenders and allowing his eyes to widen, sometimes smiling at the account of an offense, and halting the proceedings to scribble intently in a notebook of his own. Eventually the thing is done. Miss Madison, noticeably hoarse, hunches her shoulders and seems to withdraw into herself, utterly pale and spent. I am fatigued myself just from sitting and listening. But I am waiting impatiently along with everyone else to see what Mr. Gurdjieff will say or do.

A great sigh, as though the weight of the world has descended upon his shoulders.

"Have made much trouble. For self and for me."

A baleful look around the room. Another profound sigh. A despondent settling of himself in the chair.

"Punishment according to number of offenses! Who first? Patreek!"

"Here, Mr. Gurdjieff!"

Come."

Patrick emerges before the company. My heart contracts painfully at the sight of him. He must surely be terrified, but in those watchful gray eyes there is a guarded expression that shows nothing of what he is feeling. I know how fragile this composure is. I want to take his place, to take his so-called offenses upon myself. He is facing public humiliation at the hands of his enemy. I pray for him to be given strength to face his ordeal. Not for anything would I wish to see him run crying from the room.

115

Mr. Gurdjieff indicates the rug at his feet, and Patrick squats down beside the chair.

"I not remember everything. Read again."

Good God! To inflict this upon us again! To torture the unfortunate child! If I only had the strength of character (and of body) to rise up and bring this fiasco to a halt! But I am obliged to sit quietly as Miss Madison begins her recitation anew.

"Patrick Miller—has left the grounds without permission at every opportunity..."

At last it is done.

"You hear," Mr. Gurdjieff tells Patrick. "What you have to say for self? Is true? All?"

Patrick seems to hesitate for a moment and glances at Miss Madison, who is sitting quite motionless again with downcast eyes. Then he nods his head quickly.

"All true," Mr. Gurdjieff concludes. "Quel domage."

Shaking his head at Patrick, he reaches into his pockets— and extracts an enormous roll of grubby bank notes.

"Left grounds without permission. How many times? Five? Six?"

Miss Madison darts an astonished glance at him and instantly lowers her head. He moistens his thumb, peels back six notes, and laboriously extracts them from the roll.

"Winged Victory, plaster cast. How much worth?"

He looks around eagerly for a suggestion. The silence in the room is almost insupportable. Everyone's attention seems riveted on Mr. Gurdjieff's hands.

"Four. Five. Six," he peels back the notes.

"Mr. Orage's hole. How much earth in hole?" darting a wicked look at Orage who is kneeling near my chair, slightly in front of me so that I cannot see his face.

"Four. Five. Six."

And so on to the end of Patrick's offenses while the entire company hangs upon his every word and all the elaborate machinations with the bank notes—and Miss Madison's face slowly assumes a blotchy cast of the deepest red. When he comes to the culminating incident of Rachmilevich's teeth, he looks around warily and finding that the victim is not present, remarks admiringly,

"Such crime,"

And counts off a least a dozen notes. He hands a now substantial roll to Patrick and calls out peremptorily:

"Next criminal!"

And so on interminably though the offenses of the entire company, once more reiterated, in an atmosphere of excruciatingly prolonged astonishment and disbelief, until my head is ready to fall off with exhaustion and the desire to sleep. And yet I would not have left the room even if I could have done so unobtrusively, for I am both appalled and fascinated by what is unfolding, and my attention, like that of everyone else in the room, is drawn to the slight and insignificant figure of Miss Madison where she sits at the Master's right hand, her head sunk upon her narrow bony chest.

Finally the procession ceases, and there remains a single note in Mr. Gurdjieff's hands. He casts about him a wan and despairing look, until his eyes light, as though by sheer chance, upon Miss Madison.

"Directeur!"

Miss Madison raises her head. The flush of blood has receded from her face and neck, leaving her a little paler than usual, but apart from that she shows no signs of distress.

"You take," Mr. Gurdjieff says, holding out the note. "For conscientious fulfillment of obligations."

Miss Madison takes the note and folds it carefully in her palm.

"Thank you, Mr. Gurdjieff," she says, in a tone that admits not the slightest trace of irony.

In that moment my heart suddenly goes out to her. I am appalled by what Mr. Gurdjieff has done. I feel that it is an act of senseless cruelty, directed against one whose power is a mirage and who scarcely seems capable of perceiving that she has been made a fool of. I feel truly sorry for her. I even admire the composure with which she has received the insult of the single bank note, if composure it be. In spite of her impenetrable facade, she must feel the slight deeply. I remember that she is, like everyone else in the room, a human being.

And in my feelings from Mr. Gurdjieff, what ambivalence and confusion. I cannot reconcile his behavior with what I wish and need to believe about him, with the wisdom and compassion I have seen in him. And I feel too worn down, yes, too ill, for such contortions of the spirit. What I need is peace and rest and simplicity, freedom from complications. But there is no such thing this side of eternity...

And as for Patrick: the same confusion. What will he do with all that money? What will I say to him when I see him? How can I continue to accept his waiting on me without speaking my mind?

Oh! Why did Olgivanna not come tonight? Of one thing I am sure: I will never get another wink of sleep!

20 November

I was stopped short outside Mr. Gurdjieff's door by the presence of Philos, a black-and-white mongrel with short legs and an inelegant body shaped like a small keg. Orage had promised to conduct me to the interview I had requested, but my agitation of mind was such that when he did not arrive at the appointed time, I set off without him. What if I were late and Mr. Gurdjieff was engaged with someone else? I had to talk with him, to lay my difficulties before him. I had to tell him that Patrick should no longer be required to wait on me. I would say, if necessary, that I did not wish it. I did not need a chair-carrier since the cold made it impossible for me to go outside. Adèle was capable of attending to my needs. Since the incident of the false teeth—to which neither Patrick nor I had alluded—I had felt under a constraint with him, and he had seemed rather distant with me. I knew how attached to him I was, what I wished to become for him—but when an opportunity had presented itself to intervene on his behalf, to protect him from unsuitable conditions, and to afford him the loving care that he needs, I was capable of—absolutely nothing. How can an invalid, who needs so much care herself, be capable of mothering? How could I propose myself in this role and to whom? It was a pipe dream, of a piece with my dream of the Heron, of the family that Jack and I would make together. Better for Patrick not to be tied to me by an obligation he might come to resent. Then perhaps a friendship might develop in a natural way.

Philos was lying against Mr. Gurdjieff's door so that anyone entering or leaving the room would be obliged to step over him. When I attempted to reach out and knock on the door, he rose and growled softly at me. I took a quick step backward. He settled himself against the door with an indignant snort.

I was about to retrace my steps in search of Orage when the door opened suddenly and a sullen-looking Patrick appeared. He was holding a large roll of bank notes.

"Mr. Gurdjieff says for you to come in."

At the same moment I heard Mr. Gurdjieff's voice from within.

"Philos! *Attends!*"

The dog raised his head for a moment and then slowly lowered it onto his paws. His eye watched me as I stepped forward. He did not move from the doorway.

"You'll have to step over him, Mrs. Murry," Patrick said. "It's all right. He won't eat you. Give me your hand."

I fancied that there was a trace of pity in his voice. But in my distress I could not be sure of anything. He helped me into the room. Mr. Gurdjieff was seated cross-legged upon a massive bed, with a variety of objects—books, cups, handkerchiefs, papers— scattered about him among the disarray of the sheets. He was dressed in suit and overcoat, as though about to leave for one of his trips, but he wore no shoes. He smiled at me and made a gesture with his hand, as if asking me to overlook the spectacular disorder of the room.

"Sit," he said, indicating an armchair by the tall window. "Rest."

Patrick scurried ahead of me, plucking items of clothing off the floor to clear my path to the chair. I lowered myself into it and settled back, relieved to be off my feet. I had walked a long way by myself, and my breath was short. For a moment I was afraid I would start to cough. But then I remembered where I was, and this fear was overwhelmed by my nervousness at being in such close proximity to Mr. Gurdjieff.

Patrick made for the door, picking some coffee cups off the bed as he went.

"Stay," Mr. Gurdjieff said. "We will ask Mrs. Murry about your problem."

Patrick stood by the door, the cups and the money still in his hands. He looked quite uncomfortable, and I was convinced that it was on account of me. Perhaps he thought that I had come to complain about him. His presence made my task more difficult. But I was determined to carry out my intention.

I was about to speak when Mr. Gurdjieff turned to me with a huge smile. He seemed to be in an extraordinarily good humor.

"Patrick does not wish to spend the money I give him for punishments."

"Why not, Patrick?" I said, before I could help myself.

Patrick made a sullen face. Mr. Gurdjieff positively beamed, looking back and forth from Patrick to me.

"Tell," he commanded. "Tell Mrs. Murry."

"I feel sorry for Miss Madison," Patrick said, looking down at the floor.

Mr. Gurdjieff rubbed his hands together gleefully. He darted a quick glance at me, as if to see how I was taking this.

"Ask him why he feel this."

"Patrick?"

Patrick shrugged and continued to look at the floor. I began to feel terribly uncomfortable and wondered if I should get up and leave. Mr. Gurdjieff was using my presence for some purpose that I could not comprehend. I did not like it, and I felt sure that it would make Patrick dislike me all the more.

"Tell!" Mr. Gurdjieff instructed.

"I don't understand," Patrick burst out. "Why did you give me this money? All I did was to make trouble. You said so yourself!"

Mr. Gurdjieff chuckled quietly at some private source of amusement. Then he turned to me.

"What you feel?"

"I feel sorry for Miss Madison too," I told him.

He nodded, as if pleased with my answer.

"You think Patrick is good troublemaker?"

"I think he's high-spirited. He doesn't mean to make trouble."

Mr. Gurdjieff's eyes sparkled, and he laughed out loud. There was something conspiratorial about his laughter. When he was amused by you, you might take offense if you wished, but he invited you to share his amusement.

"Cannot *help* make trouble," he said decidedly, with a sly glance at Patrick. "Is very important: not everyone can do. Is very useful for me. Like yeast for making bread. Without trouble, life at Preiuré—is dead! People are like water; they seek lowest level, live mechanically, without conscience, even here. Without trouble—no chance to awake!"

He beckoned to Patrick, who returned from the door, his hair hanging in his eyes.

"This money should really be a reward from Miss Madison. Is truth! Why so? You make trouble for Miss Madison all the time. You irritate her, make her mad. But without you, her conscience will fall asleep. You help keep her *alive*. Understand?"

Patrick reached up and pushed the hair out of his eyes. He was looking at Mr. Gurdjieff with great interest.

"But it must have been awful for her," he said, "when she saw you give me the money."

Mr. Gurdjieff shook his head and chuckled.

"Feel awful, maybe," he said. "But not *just* awful. People think is necessary to talk all the time. But is possible to learn many things from feeling, only from feeling. How you feel when this happen to Miss Madison? You feel pity, no? Mrs. Murry feels pity. Yes?"

He glanced at me, and I nodded.

"Other people too. This is a new experience for Miss Madison. People say behind her back, That woman, because she is not friendly in self. People do not like her: they laugh. But the other night people do not laugh. Truth, Miss Madison feels awful, embarrassed, maybe ashamed. But many people now feel sympathy, pity, compassion, even love. She does not understand this with her mind. But she feels it—and may be her life change."

I could not deny the truth of what he said. I felt the revolution that had taken place in my own feelings for Miss Madison. As I sat there, I was ashamed of what those feelings had been. But it was a clean shame that seemed to burn them away. In their place was a feeling of sympathy for a suffering human being.

"How can her life change?" Patrick interjected. "She is still Director!"

Mr. Gurdjieff's eyes sparkled wickedly.

"Example: let us take Patreek! Last month you hate Miss Madison, no?" He assumed an absurd voice that mimicked Patrick's. "I hate Miss Madison, I dig up her flowers, I climb the wall and go to Avon—just because she tell me not to go. Now you say," (an absurdly doleful face) "I feel sorry for Miss Madison. Mr. Gurdjieff is a bad man. Why does he make her feel awful? Better to punish me instead. Truth? Now you do not hate her, you do not think she is funny. You even *like* her."

He grinned triumphantly at me. Patrick was shuffling his feet, clamping his hand to his forehead, trying unsuccessfully to conceal his pleasure at being teased.

"So is a good thing I do for Miss Madison, even if she does not know. Now she has a friend: Patreek. She will know, because you cannot hide, even if you wish. Someday she will even understand what I do, feel warm in her heart, maybe even like me for this thing. But such learning takes a long time."

The mention of time fell ominously on my ears. I was very moved by his words, which I felt were intended also for me, though addressed to Patrick. And something had changed in me, even in the short time since I had entered his room.

I became aware that there was a certain intensity that radiated from Mr. Gurdjieff: his animation, his posture, his voice. He was literally blazing with energy, I could feel it in the room, and yet he was sitting there perfectly at ease, discoursing upon a small and apparently insignificant incident. I realized that he was able to make you feel that everything in life was of supreme importance, from the loftiest of ideals to the most menial of chores.

He reached out from the bed, took Patrick by the shoulder, and shook him gently.

"Is also a good thing for you," he said. "Why so? You are young, still only a boy, you do not care about other people, care only for self. But now you feel about other person, you identify with Miss Madison and regret what you do to her. Is necessary to put self in the place of other person, of Miss Madison, of Mrs. Murry. Then you can understand and help."

He spread his hands in an eloquent gesture and turned to include me. He seemed sad.

"All people are the same," he said. "Greedy, stupid, blind. If I do a bad thing, and this bad thing makes you love other person..."

He turned to me.

"Mrs. Murry. You have a question."

"You have already answered it, Mr. Gurdjieff."

122

I rose to my feet. When I reached for the bed to steady myself, Patrick sprang to my side.

"I'll take you back," he told me.

He handed me the money and took my arm. We went out together, stepping over Philos. I did not trust myself to speak even to say goodbye to Mr. Gurdjieff.

25 November

Olgivanna came before I was up and dressed. I threw a bed-jacket around my shoulders, and she sat on the edge of the bed.

"I am wicked, Olgivanna," I said. "Terribly wicked. I shall never be able to change."

She regarded me seriously for a minute, and then her sweet smile began slowly to appear.

"Why are you smiling?"

She jumped up from the bed, went to my dressing table, and brought back a mirror, which she proceeded to hold in front of me.

"Look. You see how sweet and angelic you look?"

"You'll turn my head," I said, blushing and waving the mirror away. "There is no hope for me."

"If feeling so very wicked, you can look so sweet, your wickedness surely is not so very serious."

She seemed quite disinclined to take me seriously—or even to listen to my complaints.

"It always comes back," I said. "It will never leave me be."

"What always comes back?"

"My hatred!"

"Oh, dear."

She sat on the bed again and folded her hands upon the mirror. I lay back upon my pillows, tugging at the strings of my bed-jacket. I felt that I was behaving childishly. I was imposing upon Olgivanna's kindness. But I could not help myself.

"So there is Katherine Wicked and Katherine Sweet," she said, in a musing, playful tone of voice. "And a host of other Katherines, no doubt. But Katherine Wicked is the one who has come to visit today. Let us not turn her away. That will only make her more wicked still. Let us entertain her, humor her. Let us give her the opportunity to speak her piece. After all, she deserves a hearing as well as the others. Perhaps that is all she wants. Who is it that she hates?"

"My mother!"

It was on the tip of my tongue to confess instead what I felt about Mr. Rachmilevich—which amounted almost to hatred. But I could not; it was too absurd.

"Your mother. I see. And what has your mother done to make you hate her so? She must have done *something*."

I took a deep breath.

"I am standing on the wharf in Wellington, with my sisters and my granny and my aunt, waiting for my parents' ship to dock. It has been a long dreary wait while the doctor has come and gone in his little launch. When my parents finally come ashore, my father goes straight to my granny and my aunt. How are the children? he asks them—as though we are not standing there beside him! My mother—when she finally gets around to me—greets me thus: Well, Kathleen, I can see you're as fat as ever. I have not seen them for a whole year. I am ten years old."

A sob rises in my throat, and I cannot continue. We sit in silence while I struggle with my tears.

"This is not Katherine Wicked," Olgivanna remarks.

"No, it is Katherine Sad! Katherine Wicked has gone away. She is nowhere to be found."

"Well, she will come back."

"That is what is so awful! She will come back! Over and over again. She will never give me any peace. She is stronger than either Katherine Sweet or Katherine Sad. I feel so helpless before her."

Olgivanna was silent for such a long time that I began to think she resented my behavior. I felt myself sinking into an abyss of self-pity and despair. But then she began to talk, in a rather dispassionate way, without looking at me. She said that the road to freedom passes through the experience of complete helplessness and insignificance and there is no detour around it. What does this experience mean? It means to see that I am behaving mechanically—and that I cannot do otherwise. It means to see that I have a limited repertoire of roles—of Katherines—and that I am constrained to play one or other of them at all times. It means to sit still with that knowledge and not to try to escape from it.

There ensued the following strange dialogue:

KM: I am ashamed to tell you such things about my family. I am ashamed to *feel* as I do about them.

O: But why?

KM: It is all so sordid—and so disreputable!

O: Exactly! What did you expect?

KM: I don't know. I suppose I expected that there would be a sort of abstract state of remorse, that this was the aim of all inner efforts, the state to be looked for. It would be painful, certainly, but it would not be quite so—personal!

O: That is a mistake that I made too. I was looking for a pure and uplifting experience, devoid of unpleasant personal feelings. Perhaps the men here encourage this with all their talk about higher bodies and cosmology and so forth. I tried to suppress the personal—by which I mean all that I do not like in myself—while all the time I told myself that I was struggling with it and I called that struggle work. But it was simply a way of escaping from myself. Do not despair, Katherine. You wish to work. You wish to change. Mr. Gurdjieff likes to say: Must give the devil his due. He calls it Holy Denying Force. Why? Because we cannot work without it. You must acknowledge what is in you, what is personal to you, by being present to it without judgment. First come into possession of your own feelings, however unpleasant. As for change—the awareness itself is already a change.

KM: If I understand any part of what you say, it is that my hateful feelings about my family, my husband, about the people I have met here—Miss Madison and the English, Rachmilevich and Patrick—and even about Mr. Gurdjieff, all of this, in fact, which arises out of the person that I am, all that has to do with Katherine, as I know her, all her thoughts, feelings, and perceptions, everything that constitutes her personality is...is...

O: Is the material with which you must do your work.

KM: I feel that I cannot *stand* it, I cannot stand myself, there are things in myself that are simply nauseating to me.

O: Ah yes. I have felt this also. If we saw all at once what we are like, perhaps we *would* go mad. But it is so very hard to see ourselves, and that protects us from seeing too much too soon.

KM: But what can help me to bear it—while it *is* there?

O: You must have faith that there is something beyond the experience of helplessness. I have felt at times that something in me was going to die, that I would no longer even know myself any more. But then after this experience, there *is* something else, something stronger. It is not so hard, afterwards. You have not died. You have faced something in yourself, you have passed a milestone...

We sat in silence for a while, and I did not know if I felt better or worse.

"Now I have a confession to make to you," Olgivanna said. "I do not like pigs. In fact, I detest them! Yet I must spend a week with them, looking after them and seeing that no harm comes to them. Madame Ostrowska says that they are very intelligent and that it will be quite interesting for me to get acquainted with them. But to me they are such revolting creatures—like giant slugs! I have always avoided farmyard animals, which is probably why Mr. Gurdjieff wants me to tend to his pigs. But I do not want to. No!"

Her plaintive tone made me laugh. I could not help myself.

"Poor Olgivanna. But I have an idea! After everyone goes to bed tonight, you and I will steal out, open the gate, and chase the pigs into the road. They will wander into Avon, and someone will steal them. Then in the morning I will tell Mr. Gurdjieff that when the pigs heard that Olgivanna was to take care of them, they simply could not endure the idea of being waited on snout and hoof by a Montenegrin princess!—and so they decided to go and live in a manner more befitting their nature."

We laughed together, leaning over the bedclothes until our heads bumped lightly. Olgivanna got up with a flounce, pretending to be angry, and went to the door.

"It is all very well to laugh—but you are going to be sent to the cowshed!"

With that parting shot, she left me. I felt very much restored in spirits.

6 December: In the Cowshed.

But it was not at all dark, nor did it have an unpleasant smell, as she had feared. There were large double doors, opening onto the cows in their stalls and letting in a great deal of light, especially in the afternoon. And an opening in the gable—intended for a block and tackle, one of the men told her—that let light into the little railed-off gallery above the cows. Here she was to lie, per his instructions, and breathe the air of the place. It was all prepared for her. A steep narrow staircase ascended to the gallery, wherein had been placed two divans, one for herself and one for her visitors. What thoughtfulness! The floor of the gallery was covered with Persian carpets. The atmosphere was like that of a church—but what a homely and friendly little church, tucked away from the bustle of the house, open to shafts of pale light yet containing corners of intimate shadow, permeated with the sweet smell of the hay, the sudden rustling of the cows, the rhythm of their slow and deliberate chewing, and the silent, stately presence of the horse, Belle.

She was not lonely, even when she had no visitors, because of the cows. There were three of them, real beauties, immense and solid, with rich silky flanks and short curly wool between their horns and great eyes in which you could see your reflection. How she loved them! They were called Mitasha, Bridget, and Equivoquetecka, but everyone now referred to them collectively as Mrs. Murry's cows. How she longed for the day when she would be able to milk them!

In order to get to the stable she had to pass the pen in which Olgivanna's piglets lay sprawled beside the massive belly of the sow. There were geese in the yard, and sometimes one of them would appear momentarily in the doorway, as if to greet her. She felt herself becoming more and more absorbed in the life of the animals, and she wondered why she had always lived so far away from the natural world, even when she was yearning for it. She remembered a line from her beloved Chekhov about "the mysterious, exquisite life of nature, rich and sacred, from which we sinful mortals are shut out." There *was* such a life, going on all the time in spite of us, as it were, and in the quiet of the cowshed, especially in the late afternoon when the light began to fail, she felt herself draw near to it and was comforted.

The cows were usually milked by Madame Ostrowska. She was a little in awe of Madame O, not just because she was *his* wife, but because of her presence, of the calm authority that she exuded. She was tall and shapely and wore an old-fashioned black dress, tight in the waist and bodice, rich and full in the skirt. About her beautiful dignified head she wore a black scarf, knotted under her chin in the manner of a peasant woman. She spoke no English—indeed she was rarely heard to speak at all—but when she came to milk the cows, she never failed to acknowledge the figure lying on the divan in the little gallery above her. She would smile and gesture toward the stalls or display the milk pail that she was carrying. Frequently she would stand for a while in the doorway, as though keeping the woman above company, before she began work. The gray-blue eyes—in which there was just a touch of apprehension—looked into the distance, not vacantly, but with attention and presence: a face bearing the imprint of the experience of generations. Then she would bare graceful arms, fetch the stool from among the straw, and fall to. Her long-fingered hands began to milk, deftly, confidently, in response to an unheard rhythm. By the sounds of the milk in the pail—the thin silvery singing followed by the heavier plonk! plonk!—the woman above could tell how fast the operation was proceeding. She could see Madame O's head pressed against Equivoquetecka's flank. The cow stood perfectly still, undoubtedly in a state of exaltation. Why, the cows must experience a super-cow-sensation when Madame O milked them, if they were at all decent cows!

She knew that one day she would write a long long story about it.

On some days Adèle came to do the milking and brought her a glass of new milk from the pail. The invalid felt sure the milk would do her good because Mr. Gurdjieff had ordered it. Adèle decorated the staircase to the gallery with leaves and branches, and she would sit for a few minutes before she went back to her work. There was such tenderness in her friend's solicitude that it did not matter whether they spoke or not.

But her little boy did not come to see her. She had allowed herself to think of Patrick as *her* little boy, the very child who had been her secret companion at the Casetta, the child she had tried to draw on her letter to Jack. She knew it was wrong to think of him this way, but perhaps an invalid might be forgiven such a transparent self-deception. She was pining for him, but when she caught a glimpse of him in the kitchen or dashing through the corridors on some urgent errand, she was incapable of stopping him to ask if he would come. It was too cold to be outside, and so his chair-carrier duties were in abeyance.

One day Adèle found her in tears. She quickly sat on the floor beside the couch and touched the ruby cluster lightly with her fingers. Despite her embarrassment, the invalid was grateful.

"You miss your husband, Mrs. Murry."

"I miss the child we will never have."

She had blurted it out before she could stop herself.

"When you are well..." Adèle murmured.

"I will never be well enough to have a child," she said. "But when I am stronger I would like to adopt one. A little boy. Like Patrick."

Their eyes met. A smile of comprehension spread slowly on her companion's youthful features.

"It would be wonderful for him. But how—?"

"I will find a way."

Adèle snatched up the invalid's hand and pressed it to her lips. Her eyes were alive with excitement.

"No one must know," the invalid said. "It will be our secret."

When the sound of Adèle's steps had ceased, she fell back on her pillows. She was tired, as though after physical exertion. But she had made up her mind.

There were more good days than bad in the cowshed. And she must not forget the most marvelous thing of all! The white-washed walls and the ceiling above her couch had been decorated by Mr. Salzmann, a tall, haggard, shabbily dressed man, for all the world like a brigand with his cropped gray hair and fierce expression. He had created a kind of Persian pattern of yellow, red, and blue, with flowers, birds, butterflies, and a spreading tree with all kinds of animals peering through the branches. Was it her imagination or did she discern a resemblance between these animals and certain of the company? The elephant evoked Orage's stolid loyalty. And the ape—she could not breathe a word to anyone, not even to Olgivanna—but its comic grimace recalled an expression of Jimmy Young's. The hippopotamus!—was it not Frank Pinder in a suit of armor? And the turtle doves had surely been inspired by an engaged couple whom everyone teased because of their lack of interest in the work of the Institute. Mr. Salzmann worked lightly, playfully, and yet with real art: a little masterpiece. When she lay back to contemplate it, she felt herself surrounded by summer grasses and the kind of flowers that smell like milk. Was it possible that the loneliness and isolation of the Chalet des Sapins—where she lay waiting for her husband to come in, knowing that he knew she was waiting, painfully aware of herself as an invalid and a burden—was it possible that such a life had given place to this?

Then one afternoon a bulky shadow fell across the doorway, and *he* was standing there. She felt a little catch at her heart. He came stamping heavily up the stairway and seated himself on the other divan, leaning toward her in the most companionable way, as though it were a long-established custom for them to sit together in the dusk of the cowshed without speaking. After a while he began to talk about the cows, their personalities, their merits and their idiosyncrasies, with the most elaborate seriousness, and all the time his eyes sparkled as he watched her to see if she appreciated his drollery. He had bought a little monkey that was to be trained to clean the cows. It seemed an improbable sort of idea, but he spoke about it in such a matter-of-fact way that she had no doubt it would come to pass. Then suddenly he asked her how she was and without waiting for an answer declared that she looked better. Immediately she felt that she was better.

"Now!" he said. "You have two doctors you must obey. Doctor Cowshed and Doctor New Milk. Have traveled much. Now rest. This your task. Not to think. Not to write. Live in the body again."

Two goats were installed in the cowshed. They were very lovely as they lay below her in the straw or delicately danced around each other, butting their heads gently. They were Nubian goats, and she was fascinated by the strange square pupil of the eye; it seemed somehow a violation of the natural order of things.

When he came again, Adèle was there, and he proceeded to show her how to milk the goats. He sat on the stool, seized one of the goats, and swung its hind legs across his knees, so that it was supported only on its front legs and was therefore quite helpless. This was the way Arabs milked, and he looked very like one, squatting on the stool, with his shaved head and powerful thighs and shoulders. Adèle stood behind him and cast a look of consternation into the gallery. Then it was her turn. The goat escaped from her, and he had to retrieve it. Finally she got the knack of it. He watched her for a while and professed himself satisfied.

When Adèle had left with her half-filled pail, he came up the stairs and sat on the divan. Philos followed him and flopped down at his feet. He tugged at its ears, and it tried halfheartedly to bite his hand. Grinning he watched it for a while until it began to whine. Then he hushed it and turned to her.

"You like the stable? Is better than the Ritz?"

"I love it here," she said, grateful for the opportunity to show her appreciation. "I feel that it is better for me to breathe the air of this cowshed than to have the attentions of all the doctors in the world! And I love to be near the animals."

It was a long speech for her, and her excitement made her a little breathless. He continued to look down at the dog, which was now resting its muzzle on his boot.

"Dog and horse are special animals," he said. "Especially dog. Hey, Philos? Is necessary to treat with kindness."

He looked up at her.

"With kindness," he repeated. "Comes from kin, family, the same kind. Means to treat like self."

He tilted back his head until he was looking at Mr. Salzmann's bestiary and remained in this attitude for at least a minute.

"Man is a three-centered being," he said finally, "with body, mind, and heart. Animals have only two centers, cannot acquire a third brain and become like man. But for this reason, is necessary always to treat with kindness. Because even though he knows that he cannot become like man, in his heart a dog—and horse and sometimes cow—who associates with man *wishes* to become like man. Is very sad thing to wish for the impossible. You look at dog and you always see in his eyes this sadness—because he knows is not possible for him, but still he wishes. And all because of man. Man has corrupted dog by trying to make him human. For this reason," (he paused to look in her eyes), "always be kind."

She felt the tears come because he had articulated something she had always sensed, the sadness in the eyes of the so-called dumb animal, and the embarrassment she had felt in the presence of some of her friends' pets, the feeling that here was a creature degraded by its contact with humans.

"I have two cats," she whispered. "Wingley and Athenaeum. But I have never felt—"

He waved his hand dismissively.

"Cat is different, has respect for self. If you try to mistreat, cat will bite or scratch or run away. Is proper for cat to be like that. Cannot be spoiled by man. But cannot wish either, like old dog."

He got to his feet with a sigh and padded away over the carpets, Philos at his heels.

But sometimes she was depressed, even in the company of the cows. It was intensely cold in the mornings in her bare little servant's room, and although she hardly noticed the disorder of the house, she was longing for some real change—and for beauty. She had almost decided to ask him to let her go away until the weather got warmer. She had not confided to anyone what she was thinking, not even to Olgivanna, certainly not to Jack. She knew in advance what Olgivanna would say: to reveal her lack of faith to Olgivanna would be to vanquish the idea of leaving. But it would be an empty victory, since she would not have come to it of herself. What was to be done? She could summon Ida to her: Ida would come. But where would they go and under what conditions? How would they live with each other? It was impossible. And how could she bear a separation from Patrick? She would stay because she had no choice. It was the only course open to her, and therefore no credit was due to her for having chosen it.

His appearance in the doorway only made her feel the more miserable, as though he might be able to guess at the traitorous thoughts that were going through her mind. He took his seat on the divan as usual.

"You have a question?"

She became terribly agitated, and her mind was a complete blank. She needed help—but what kind of help? She could not think what to say to him.

"You *wish* for something?" he murmured.

What did she wish for? She had to think. No, that was not the way. She had to allow the answer to come to her from her whole being. For she *did* wish, of that she was sure, with some deeper, surer part of herself that was below or beyond all the coming and going, all the petty traffic of her mind.

"Imagine God can hear. What you ask for?"

"If I were to be allowed one single prayer," she said deliberately, "that prayer would be, I want to be *real*."

He gave a little grunt and shifted in his seat. Was it the right answer? No matter. It was the one that had come to her. It was what she wished for above all things now, to know that her impulses came from that deeper, surer part of herself, from Katherine True rather than Katherine False. But how could that be attained?

"Must *learn* to pray," he said, "just as with everything. We think is only one kind of prayer: we ask God, and He grants—or He does not grant. But real prayers have nothing to do with asking; real prayers are repetitions. Repeat aloud or to self. Try to experience with whole of mind and feeling and even body. Only in this way can you benefit from prayer."

She felt herself relax. She was sure that he was about to help her.

"You say, 'I want to be real' or 'I want to remember myself.' Is a prayer. But how do you say? If you say even ten thousand times and are thinking of your mother or how soon you will finish and what will be for dinner, then is not prayer but merely sleep. Must say like this: 'I.' And at the same time try to think what you know about 'I.' Does not exist, is no single 'I,' is a multitude of small 'I's that cannot agree. But you want to be one 'I,' to be master. 'Want': what means to want? Are you *able* to want? With you 'it wants' or 'it does not want' all the time. Always 'it,' never 'I.' Must oppose 'it' with your own 'I want,' which is connected to aim of your work, to your reason for being here. 'To remember.' Must think about memory. How little we remember. How often we forget what we have decided, what we have seen, what we know! Life would be different if we could remember. All ills come because we do not remember. 'Myself.' Come back to self. But which self? Which self you wish to remember? How can you distinguish between them? Which self can help you to work?"

He ceased, sighed, hunched over his knees, as though preparing to rise. She felt that something tangible had passed from him to her. He had given her a prayer. He had *said* a prayer for her.

"You will remember to say sometimes?"

She nodded eagerly, smiling her gratitude upon him.

"Oh, yes! Thank you. I have so *much* time, and I do not do anything, except lie around."

"You pray to God," he said. "But what is God? Where is He now? How will He know you are praying? How will He ever think of you, take notice of you?"

She had a moment of consternation. But he went on:

"I wish to remember myself. Is necessary to think when saying each word. And then—if you think—is precisely your thoughts can do for you what you ask God to do."

He got up and went to the head of the stairs.

"Return to Ritz tomorrow," he said. "I tell Olgivanna."

9 December

My fortunes have changed. I have been returned to the beautiful room overlooking the park that I first occupied when I came here more than a month ago. I can hardly believe that such grandeur is again at my disposal. But I think I have learned the lesson that the other room had to teach me. I have learned that I can rough it as I never have before, that I can put up with noise, untidiness, disorder, and even the close proximity of people one does not know without losing my head or suffering more than superficially. This is the real revelation: that much of my suffering is superficial, unnecessary, inessential. It seems absurd to say so, but I had become attached to it, almost fond of it, as a sort of habit, an identity, a way of being in the world. Now it falls away. Leaving that which is inescapable...And necessary?

Mr. Gurdjieff has thrown the whole community into a new project: the construction of a building he calls the Study House. After extremely strenuous work, a very large area at the edge of the forest has been cleared, and upon this site the residents are raising the frame of an old aircraft hanger that Mr. Gurdjieff has acquired "on the cheap." The area is the scene of an ongoing scurry party, and the work proceeds all day and into the night, I am told, for Mr. Gurdjieff is determined that the first performance of the dances will take place in the Study House on the thirteenth of January, his birthday. The uprights of the building are already in place; the space between the rough laths is stuffed with dead leaves and covered over with the material out of which the Hebrews made bricks for their Egyptian slave masters, a mixture of mud and straw. It is all very unorthodox; some of the men have expressed concern that the building, if it is ever completed, will not be able to support its own weight.

This morning, the weather being unseasonably warm, I went to watch the work in progress, escorted by Patrick in the capacity of my chair carrier. I was delighted to have him with me again, and I kept stealing little glances at him until he noticed and turned upon me his full searching gaze. I returned the look, my heart overflowing, until he moved away—not without an endearing little grin that made my spirits soar. My chair was placed outside the framework so that I could watch without being in the way. It seemed that the entire community was assembled inside the maze of uprights, working so closely together that they trod on one another's heels. Some were engaged in fabricating the walls, others were traversing the enclosed area with heavy iron rollers to create a smooth surface for a floor, while a few fearless souls moved about on the girders overhead. Mr. Gurdjieff marched up and down among them, whispering a word to one, shouting at another, seizing an implement to demonstrate what he wanted, and generally whipping his troops in a frenzy of activity. The energy of the project seemed to emanate from his relentless will; one had the impression that if he were to leave the scene, the entire proceedings, including the framework, would simply fall to the ground.

As I watched, my attention was drawn to one of the workers overhead, a member of the Russian contingent, to whom I had never spoken. He was sitting in the angle formed by two beams, about twenty feet above the ground, very still and relaxed, with his eyes closed and his tools resting in his lap. I realized to my horror that he was asleep. I looked around frantically for someone who could give the alarm. But before I could open my mouth, Mr. Gurdjieff rushed forward with a ladder, placed it against the upright, mounted nimbly to the sleeping man, gripped him firmly by the shoulder and pressed him back against the vertical support. The man's eyes popped open, and he looked at Mr. Gurdjieff in astonishment. For a moment Mr. Gurdjieff spoke urgently at his ear. Then he descended, leaving the man shaking his head ruefully.

Mr. Rachmilevich, who rarely took part in any of the projects or scurry parties, was filling in the hole in which one of the uprights had been placed. My eyes were drawn involuntarily to his sour expression and the continual movement of his lips, as he muttered to himself. Truly, my ill feeling for him was irresistible. As much as I tried to turn my mind away, there was something in me that positively rejoiced when I saw him because of this opportunity to indulge myself.

As soon as Mr. Gurdjieff stepped down from the ladder and resumed his prowl among the workers, Mr. Rachmilevich flung his spade to the ground with great violence, planted himself in the master's path, and began to shout at the top of his voice. I assumed that he was shouting in Russian since I could not understand a word; he was so incensed as to be actually frothing at the mouth. Everyone downed tools at once and turned to watch. Even the man sitting on the girder peered down, alert and fascinated. Rachmilevich waved his arms, pointing first to the man above, then to the uprights that supported him, then to the rest of the company. Mr. Gurdjieff had come to a halt and stood quietly and attentively, his face impassive, his eyes fixed upon the figure of Rachmilevich who was jerked hither and thither like a puppet by his uncontrollable rage.

The gaunt figure of Mr. Salzmann, the painter, strolled toward me. He was a member of the Russian contingent and as such a long-standing associate of Mr. Gurdjieff's whom he treated with easy familiarity. He was also the friend of Chekhov's widow, Olga Knipper, according to Orage, and this had drawn me to him. But I was put off by his offhand manner and unkempt appearance until one day he sat down beside me during a scurry party and we had had a great talk about Chekhov's work.

Mr. Salzmann stopped to lean upon the back of my chair.

"Rachmilevich says that what we are doing is insane," he remarked nonchalantly. "Sooner or later an accident will occur when Georgivanitch is not there to prevent it. Someone will break his neck. Or if by some miracle this Study House is constructed without loss of life, then it will collapse at the first puff of wind and kill us all—with the exception of Georgivanitch who will attribute the calamity to a failure to follow his instructions."

Rachmilevich ceased, presumably to catch his breath, and to my amazement Mr. Gurdjieff commenced to berate him with a fury that was overwhelming. He was the very embodiment of rage, and he seemed to grow in stature until he appeared to be looming over the unfortunate Rachmilevich, who was actually taller than he. The enormity of his anger was such that I felt that if this appalling scene were prolonged I would not be able to endure it. Something in me would simply break.

Beside me Mr. Salzmann murmured:

"Georgivanitch says that he has been unjustly criticized before the entire house, that he knows better than anyone else in the world the forces that act upon such buildings, that he has constructed them in a dozen different countries and never has one fallen upon him or anyone else, that he is in fact the foremost living expert in all the West and a great part of the East upon such construction—and who is Rachmilevich to call his authority into question?"

I turned my head to look at him. Something in his kind, exhausted eyes reassured me.

"And so on. And so forth," he said, with the faint shadow of a smile.

I turned back to the confrontation. I found that I was able to observe what was going on, instead of being overwhelmed by it. Mr. Gurdjieff was still pouring forth invective effortlessly. To Rachmilevich's credit, he stood his ground, his eyes fixed on Mr. Gurdjieff, his expression scornful rather than frightened. In fact, he seemed to be watching for an interruption in the diatribe so that he could launch a counter-attack.

Into this grotesque play—the audience of figures leaning on their tools, the two protagonists, the sound of Mr. Gurdjieff's voice that seemed to have a physical presence of its own—came Patrick, carrying a demitasse on a saucer. He did not appear to be concerned about what was going on. All of his attention was concentrated on the brimming cup and on where he was placing his feet. He entered the shell of the building. Several people stepped out of his path, and he walked right up to the raging Gurdjieff, his eyes still fastened upon the demitasse. He stood there and calmly waited for Mr. Gurdjieff to notice him; he was like someone who had been granted invisibility in order to participate in the spectacle without coming to harm.

Abruptly Mr. Gurdjieff's outburst ceased. Patrick slowly extended his hand, offering the cup. Mr. Gurdjieff turned to him, took the cup, and gave him his extraordinary smile, so incredibly peaceful and composed that it was impossible to believe it followed upon such a display of anger. And then that anger recommenced, as though he had thrown a switch to release it. The transformation was so rapid that I wondered for an instant if I had really seen him smile. I no longer thought that he had lost his self-possession. But the idea that he was very much in control of such an awesome power was even more astounding than that he was himself controlled by it.

The tirade came to an end at last. Rachmilevich raised his clenched fists above his head, as though invoking the assistance of higher powers, then turned on his heel and stalked away. He continued to wave his arms about, and fragments of his jeremiad floated back to us as he crossed the wide expanse of the lawns and disappeared into the woods beyond, a tiny blackened figure, his limbs still jerking like an agitated spider.

Mr. Gurdjieff appeared to rediscover the cup of coffee in his hands and raised it to his lips. Then he replaced it in the saucer and glanced about him indignantly.

"Skorey! Skorey!"

The work was resumed, if anything at a more frenetic pace than before. Patrick came toward me, suppressing a smile that lingered in his eyes. I became aware that I wore a frown of disapproval. Why? I had scarcely any right to talk since a part of me took pleasure in Mr. Rachmilevich's ignominious departure, but I could not bear to see Patrick consumed by the same unsavory emotions. My throat felt suddenly constricted, and tears came to my eyes. I watched him laughing at a remark addressed to him by Mr. Salzmann, tossing the hair out of his eyes and clapping his hand to the crown of his head. I loved him so much. I wished with all my heart for him to be well and happy. But a little voice continued to whisper to me, Why should he care for the likes of *you*?

Patrick arrived at my chair at the same time as—Mr. Gurdjieff. The two of them exchanged a look and then turned to me, as though I had summoned them. Mr. Gurdjieff had assumed an ingenuous expression of complete mystification, and I couldn't help smiling.

"State your business," I said to both of them.

Mr. Gurdjieff leaned toward me confidentially and motioned Patrick to do the same.

"Is a great misfortune," he said ruefully. "We must find Mr. Rachmilevich and bring him back. Is necessary for the work."

He gestured toward the toiling workers behind him.

"It seems to me, Mr. Gurdjieff, that Mr. Rachmilevich is more of an impediment to the work than anything else—when he consents to work at all."

He eyed me seriously for a moment and then slowly shook his head.

"Is a very old friend. We must find a way for him to return and still save face."

He turned abruptly to Patrick.

"You go and persuade him to come back."

"Me?" Patrick gasped. "Why me?"

"You," Mr. Gurdjieff said conclusively. "No good if I go. He will not listen."

"But what will I say to him?"

"You will think of what to say. Wait one hour, eat lunch, digest. Wait till he is not so angry, till his stomach tells him he should come back."

"But I don't know where he is," Patrick moaned. "How will I find him?"

"This your task. Think what he will do. Then you will find. Take horse. Perhaps horse will help."

"He won't listen to me. He hates me."

But I could tell that Patrick's heart was no longer in his complaint. He loved to be allowed to take care of the horse, even more than the chickens or the dog.

"Take Mrs. Murry," Mr. Gurdjieff said. "She will help too. Harness horse to wagon. Eat, rest. Then go."

And so it happened that an hour later I found myself seated beside Patrick on the little wagon proceeding bumpily across the lawn. It was with some trepidation that I had agreed to the excursion, but I felt restored by lunch and by the gallant company of Mr. Salzmann who had helped me to climb into the wagon and stood by to see us off. The day was still warm, the sky cloudless, and the spring-like scent that rose from the earth created a strange excitement in me, though it sorted ill with the leafless branches of the trees.

We entered the forest and creaked slowly down a narrow dirt track. Sunlight flickered on the great glossy rump of the horse plodding between the shafts—and I felt joy bubbling up within me, the joy of what my senses brought me: the gently rocking motion of the wagon, the play of light and shade, the exquisite aromas released by the unseasonable warmth, and Patrick sitting beside me, gripping the reins, made serious by his responsibilities.

"She prefers the wagon to having someone ride her," he informed me.

"How do you know?"

"I just know," he stated, matter-of-factly. "She likes to be of use to us, even if she is old."

"Did she tell you this?" I teased.

"I know her better than anyone," he said seriously. "She likes to be rubbed down, but only so much, and then you must stop or it is all spoiled for her. She likes you to be quiet when you first come in and before you go out. She likes to be scratched on the withers. And when I graze her on the lawn, she likes to use *me* as a scratching post!"

"Is she going to find Rachmilevich for us?"

"I don't know. Are you, Belle?"

The horse tossed her head and peered back at us out of one huge liquid eye.

"She will find him if he is some place where she can go," Patrick informed me. "Unless he's gone to Paris."

"Do you think he has?"

Patrick assumed a serious expression. It was obvious that he was thinking about what Mr. Gurdjieff had said.

"No. He would not leave without his belongings. Or his cigarettes. He smokes like a chimney. He would need at least two packs for the train to Paris."

"Perhaps he has gone to Avon."

"No. He doesn't like to go there. He thinks that people are talking behind his back, calling him a *fou* because he lives at the Prieuré."

"And are they?"

"Sure," Patrick grinned. "They think the Prieuré is a *maison de fous*! But nobody here cares, except for Rachmilevich."

We trundled on. Patrick was confiding in me, and I was elated. I felt that I had gone over to his side, that I had given up all pretense to being a parent—or an adult for that matter. I was his co-conspirator, his fellow-adventurer. It gave me a delicious sense of freedom from constraint, of simple unaffected joy in his company. And after all, surely children have need of adult companions who will meet with them on their own terms, who will take their concerns seriously, who will descend to their level. I am not so sure it is really a descent.

After a delightful journey of about a mile, we emerged into one of the remote vegetable gardens at the boundary of the property. And there we beheld Mr. Rachmilevich—sitting among the branches of an apple tree!

"Hah!" Patrick exclaimed. "Maybe he *is* mad!"

He brought Belle to a halt, and we sat there and looked at Mr. Rachmilevich. He had his back to us and gave no sign that he was aware of our presence, though he could not have failed to hear the wagon. The scene had a dream-like quality: the deep shadow of the woods from which we had emerged, the closed beds of the garden surrounded by pale yellow grasses, a sky of the palest blue, and over all the profound expectant silence of the sleeping earth. The black form of Mr. Rachmilevich sat spider-like in the tangle of the tree, his skinny legs looped about a limb while his hands clutched the branches above him. It must have been a peculiar temperament that sought such a bizarre expression of its distress. But I could not feel the slightest sympathy.

"What will I say to him, Mrs. Murry?" Patrick whispered.

"Tell him Mr. Gurdjieff says he is to come back," I answered, with a conviction I did not feel. "They have set aside some lunch for him in the kitchen."

"He'll eat *me*."

"Not if I can help it, Patrick," I said.

"Mr. Gurdjieff has turned him into a crow!" Patrick giggled. "The King of the Crows. All he needs is a crown for his head and some feathers."

I turned away to conceal a smile. Patrick gave a little yelp of suppressed laughter.

"Let us go and talk to him," I said.

Patrick flicked the reins, and Belle advanced until the wagon was positioned directly beneath the limb upon which Mr. Rachmilevich was poised. We both peered up at him. He did not seem to be particularly surprised to see us. He cast one disdainful glance downward and then averted his eyes, staring off into the ruddy western sky. With his sparse scattered locks of gray hair and haggard visage, he looked like a man who longed for night to fall and bring an end to the tribulations of the day.

"We are here to take you back, Mr. Rachmilevich," Patrick called out in an comically deferential tone, emphasizing the 'we', as though he was aware that there was safety in numbers. "Mr. Gurdjieff sent us."

"I am not coming back," Mr. Rachmilevich pronounced, slowly and with excessive dignity, without looking down.

He did not seem to have any particular reaction to my presence on the scene, which relieved me. I was obviously of no interest to the man, which I could scarcely complain of in the light of my aversion for him. And yet I received his indifference as a sort of slight. I could not understand my reaction. I only knew that I was acutely nervous in his presence, and that this nervousness clouded my understanding and prevented me from knowing why he was so odious to me.

"What will we say to Mr. Gurdjieff?" Patrick persisted.

"You may tell Georgivanitch—" Mr. Rachmilevich began hastily, then shot a fearful glance at me, and ceased. "Tell him I intend to leave this place."

"Please come down, Mr. Rachmilevich. What if you were to fall?"

Mr. Rachmilevich's mouth set in a hard line. He did not reply. Patrick glanced at me and made a face.

"He's in a ferocious mood," he hissed.

I glanced up. There was something pathetic about the way Mr. Rachmilevich's legs dangled from the branch, the narrow legs of his trousers drawn up almost to his knees. I didn't not think he looked particularly ferocious. If anything, he was the embodiment of helpless, unrepentant misery.

"We will wait for you, Mr. Rachmilevich," Patrick trilled. "We can't go back without you. What will Mr. Gurdjieff say?"

Patrick leaned toward me confidentially.

"My grandfather told me that when the saints of Ireland wanted something from the king, they sat outside his door and went on hunger strike. Sometimes they were there for weeks. Sometimes they died! It was a great disgrace for the king."

I did not relish the prospect of waiting out Mr. Rachmilevich, not to mention fasting in order to procure his compliance. The sun had set behind the trees, and the cold breath of winter enveloped us. I was tired and longing for the comfort of my room. But I was also caught up in Patrick's excited sense of responsibility. We had been charged to bring Mr. Rachmilevich back. Indeed I myself felt that his demeanor, if it did not indicate madness, certainly gave grounds for concern. We would not be acting in his best interests were we to leave him in his roost without food or drink, at close of day, in an obviously agitated state of mind. I set my teeth (to keep them from chattering), pulled my fur coat more closely around me, and folded my arms tightly upon my chest. The struggle had begun. Which of us would yield?

Patrick pulled the wagon forward so that Mr. Rachmilevich was suspended over the rear of it and we were no longer obliged to stare into his disagreeable face. He let the reins hang loose, and Belle bent her neck to the grasses at her feet. We exchanged a knowing look. On the face of it, we were two ill-assorted persons who had been sent on an unpleasant errand. But since we both knew that we were imitating the practice of the saints of old Ireland in order to preserve our honor and bring about the conversion of a reprobate, the occasion was invested with significance, and our discomfort seemed a small price in the light of our possible success.

And in the space of a mere fifteen minutes, victory was ours. I felt a jolt and realized that Mr. Rachmilevich had dropped from his tree into the wagon behind us. I cast a swift glance behind me. Mr. Rachmilevich was sitting on the end of the wagon, his legs dangling over the edge, his arms braced on either side to hold himself in place. It was impossible to speculate upon his state of mind, but his head was bowed as though reflectively, and he seemed quite subdued, no longer disposed to fight or fly. Patrick and I eyed each other warily, and I gestured toward the reins. As soon as Patrick touched them, Belle raised her beautiful head and began to move. Patrick turned her slowly and carefully, staring all the while at Rachmilevich's hunched shoulders, his face contorted in a comical frown. Then we were back on the track, proceeding through the darkened woods in silence. We did not exchange a word until Patrick drew the wagon to a halt beside the kitchen door. Mr. Rachmilevich slipped off the wagon and glided to the door like a wraith, his shabby black suit merging with the dusk. Patrick and I proceeded to the main entrance where I discerned the elegant figure of Mr. Salzmann, apparently waiting to conduct me to my room. I could tell he wished very much to know what had transpired, but I was too utterly exhausted to do more than murmur my thanks as he took an aristocratically formal leave of me at my door.

The following day I caught a glimpse of Mr. Rachmilevich at breakfast—and again at lunch. If he was planning to leave, he was not in a hurry. He looked no more disagreeable than usual.

In the afternoon I received a visit from Mr. Gurdjieff in the cowshed. He ascended the stairs with his usual heavy tread and seated himself opposite me. I knew that Patrick would have reported to him the outcome of our expedition, but somehow I did not expect him to refer to it. However, his first words were to ask if I had been surprised to see Rachmilevich at lunch.

"Indeed I *was* surprised," I said. "When he informed Patrick and me that he intended to leave the Prieuré, he seemed quite determined."

Mr. Gurdjieff was silent for a while, staring down upon the cows.

"Mr. Rachmilevich is very rich merchant in Paris," he said.

My face must have registered my incredulity.

"You do not believe," he said, "but is truth. I pay him to stay here. He is very important for my purposes. Make more trouble even than Patreek, without which is no work. But he does not want to stay, and I have to eat humble pie" (grinning mischievously) "and beg him to make sacrifice for my sake. He agrees to do, and now I am under obligation to him—for life! Is necessary, because without Rachmilevich, the Prieuré is not the same."

He turned to me, and his smile faded.

"Is also a privilege for Rachmilevich, though he does not know. Nowhere else can his personality perform such useful work, make trouble for people, give them opportunity to work. This he does naturally, without conscious effort. He cannot work on himself, is unable to change.

It seemed to me a curious fate, at best, and I was moved to say so.

"Is necessary to know all types of people," he said, looking at me intently. "Especially people you do not like. Is necessary to feel responsibility toward such people, to regard as your neighbor. Try to put self in position of neighbor. He has the same significance as you, has wishes and desires that are dear to him, that he will lose at death."

Something in me offered an instinctive objection to his words. Put yourself in the place of another? Yes, but it is impossible! Each person has the same significance? Theoretically, yes, but in point of fact I had not succeeded in discovering the significance of my own life, not to mind Mr. Rachmilevich's. What were his secret and cherished desires—unless he wanted no more than to be liked and accepted in the motley little community that Gurdjieff had created? That was what I wanted too, at bottom. But if that were the case, if our desires were not so dissimilar, then it followed that...No, it was nonsense, it was asking too much. It was an ideal that Christ himself could not live up to!

"At present you cannot see," Mr. Gurdjieff informed me. "But if you realize that he suffers like you, that he must die without attaining what is dear to him, just like you, then you will have pity and compassion toward him instead of anger and resentment, you will be just toward him in your thoughts, and finally you will love him."

I was staggered. It was as though he had read my mind. And yet I had never confided to anyone, not even to Olgivanna, how I felt about Mr. Rachmilevich.

"Did you say love, Mr. Gurdjieff?"

He waved his hand dismissively, got to his feet, and trudged away.

12 December: The Bad Day

Her friend had come in early and helped her to dress and stayed to straighten out the room. But she did not gossip or chatter about the pigs, and there was an excessive care in the way in which she handled things, as though she was holding some unexpressed feeling in check. And the invalid knew what it was. Her friend wished to escape from the sickroom, to be released from the servitude into which she had been drawn, to take her place in the community again. The invalid wished with all her heart for her friend to go. But when she spoke, she heard in her own voice her loneliness and her fear of being alone.

"It is a bad day," she said. "So gray and cold. I have never been so cold. I feel that I will never again be entirely warm."

It was not cold in the room, though the fire was burned down. She meant that something within her was losing warmth, that she was watching it slowly leach away, powerless to stop it. But her friend said:

"I will go and bring you more wood."

"Oh no, there is plenty."

"Are you sure? I want to do something for you. If only I could make the sun shine..."

"Quite sure, thank you. There is nothing I need, nothing I want that I can have."

In her friend's place she would have felt the same thing, the thing that Jack had felt, the thing that came between them. It was intolerable to be shut up with someone who was sick, who would never be well. One longed to shake off the constraint, if only for a time, to feel the heedless life of one's own body, and to forget all sickness and ill-health. She must tell her to go then; they would both feel better. But she did not want to be alone.

Her friend stooped, placed a log on the fire, and warmed her hands. Then she turned to the bed and looked straight into the invalid's eyes. "Katherine, do you mind if I go out to the Study House? I want to work there for a while."

The invalid could not meet her eyes.

"No, indeed. Why shouldn't you go?" In another minute she would cry—but her friend was gone. To run away from her with such indecorous haste. The tears came and she let them fall. It was too much to ask of any friend, to bear with her day after day. But oh! today of all days, a bad day, an evil day, when she felt so undefended, when a great waste of nothingness seemed to open out before her soul and she longed for the merest distraction. No one could have been a better friend to her

146

than Olgivanna, Mr. Gurdjieff's instructions notwithstanding. Olgivanna was more loving and devoted in her way than Ida, stronger by far in confronting the reality of the situation than Jack. She spent all her nights in the invalid's room, sitting on the little stool by the fire, listening to a recitation of the invalid's fears that could be silenced only by sleep. Olgivanna had been up early, she had worked hard all day, but she came because the invalid could not sleep unless there was someone to sit with her. It was more than one had a right to expect. But Olgivanna had borne it—until today.

The invalid got out of bed, drew a blanket about her shoulders, and sat at the writing desk before the window. Once there she surprised herself by picking up a pencil and writing on a piece of stationery:

I should like this to be accepted as my testament.

Is there no limit to the suffering that one human being is asked to bear? One thinks, Now I have touched bottom, I can go no deeper. And then one goes deeper. But I do not wish to die without leaving a record of my belief that suffering can be overcome. What to do? There is no question of "passing beyond it." That is false. One must submit. Accept it fully. Make it part of life.

But what does it mean, to make it part of life? I have always tried to thrust all forms of suffering away from me, to escape my misery in all of the innumerable ways by which people distract themselves: society, art, love—and hate. I know that suffering is inescapable, that each one receives his portion, great or small. But I have always behaved as though an exception would be made in the case of KM, I alone would not have to bear my burden, I would escape from it through the company of dear friends, through my writing, through the love I would share with Jack and our child. Sometimes that love was the assurance that Jack and I were special, singled out, spared the vicissitudes of the common lot. My illness then seemed like some malevolent thing, mustering its forces against me in darkness and mystery, implacably opposed to my bright destiny. And little by little it convinced me that there could be no bright destiny, no exemption from pain, no escape from suffering...

When I was a girl of twelve or thirteen, a friend with whom I had quarreled sent me a series of very hurtful letters. No doubt their cruelty was unconscious and childish, but they affected me deeply. I could not stop them from coming, nor could I forbear from reading them. I took my distress to my Grandma. What was I to do? I thrust the pile of letters into her lap. She let her fingers rest upon them gently, not looking at them, smiling faintly. I will give you a beautiful box, child, that my mother gave me, she said. Put each letter in it as it comes. That will take the harm out of them—and remind you to be happy in yourself no matter what anybody says.

Everything in life that we really accept undergoes a change. Suffering must become Love. To welcome suffering as one would welcome a guest, to sit down to sup with her, to wish for no other companion. To live this visitation for the space of a single breath, to wait with patience for the next breath in which one can be present to it again, even if it takes an hour, a morning, an entire day. To embrace this suffering until it should pass—for nothing lasts forever, not even suffering. Only in this way will I grow stronger.

Separateness is our most cherished illusion. How we strive to protect it. And what a relief it must be to relinquish it. To feel, to know, I do not have to bear it alone. A plague of lighthouse keepers, according to Mr. Salzmann, each one marooned upon the height of his tower, diligently tending his light, believing it to be the only light, knowing nothing of the Light that nourishes all lamps. That Light is Love. To acknowledge it is to let all defenses fall, to turn one's unprotected face to the sun.

To make an end as did my beloved Chekhov, a good man, pure of heart, although no church has seen fit to canonize him, a kind of saint. I see him as Gorky did—Chekhov standing before a crowd of the Russian people, saying in his quiet and unassuming manner, "You live badly, my friends. It is not good to live like this." How should one live? How should one die? From the point of view of life, his last letters are terrible: the world has dwindled to a ruined stomach and a shortness of breath that obliges him to lie motionless, in a state of complete helplessness, much like mine. But it is hard—it is hard to make a good death.

How did the good doctor face it? "It's such a long time since I drank champagne." To sip the parting glass and then to smile, to turn to the wall, to put Life away like a toy that one has grown tired of. To leave life on this earth as Chekhov left it. Oh! he is the one good man that I have known.

She wrote this. She looked up. The bare trees were moving in the garden, the sky was pale, she found herself weeping.

Came a sudden knock to the door. Her heart leaped. It was her friend returning.

"Come in!" she cried.

The haggard face of Mr. Rachmilevich, his lips stretched in a grimace that must have been intended for a smile, appeared around the door.

"Excuse me, Mrs. Merry,"—it was the first time she had heard him speak in English—"there is something you need today?"

His accent was so thick that some time elapsed before she comprehended what he was saying to her.

It was evening when her friend returned. She could tell who it was from the contrite sound of her knock. She was still sitting at her writing desk in a daze of exhaustion. Her friend stood by the door. "How have you been?"

"Very well. Splendid." She heard the note of false pride in her own voice. "Just fine."

Her friend looked away, as though embarrassed for her. "Who brought you the wood?"

The invalid laughed, a short mirthless laugh. "Who do you think has been to see me? Mr. Rachmilevich. It seems that I have quite won him over by bringing him back to the fold. I had quite a charming conversation with him. At least I *think* it was charming; I must admit I do not understand him very well. But I talked to him for a long time. It was most instructive."

O: What did you discover?

KM: That he is a human being, like the rest of us.

O: And you no longer felt the same dislike of him?

KM: I am embarrassed to say that I still dislike him!

O: Why should you be embarrassed? We are all the same: You, me, Rachmilevich, Miss Madison. We cannot help what we feel. But we can sit with it until—

KM: Yes, that is just it! I disliked him just as much as ever, even when he was fetching wood for my fire. But my dislike of him—didn't matter. I didn't let it upset me; it was just what I happened to be feeling. In a way it has nothing to do with Mr. Rachmilevich, since it is in me, it is my responsibility. So I sat and talked with him and did not mind how long he stayed. In fact I was sorry when he left. I did not feel so lonely while he was here. I allowed him to give me some comfort.

They were both smiling.

"Katherine, you are wonderful. Will you forgive me?"

149

The invalid felt a sudden painful contraction of the heart. "Forgive you? My guilt before you is much greater. I must confess. I complained about you to Mr. Rachmilevich. He wanted to hear or to say something disagreeable; that is his vocation. And I wanted to escape from my own pain by hurting you in some way. I told him I was cold because you left me without any wood. Will you forgive me?"

She saw the stricken look on her friend's face.

"Oh, don't you know how much I love you?" she cried. "This has been the most terrible day I have passed since I came here—and all because you were not here to keep me company."

Olgivanna sighed and made a gesture with her hand as though to dismiss the subject. "Let us forget it then. It was a bad day for both of us. Let's not mention it again."

"Oh no," the invalid said, feeling her eyes fill with tears, "I want to hear what has happened to you, what you are feeling. I know I am undeserving, but please do not shut me out of your confidence. Not today. Please!"

Her friend came and sat in the window and took the invalid's hands across the desk. "Today I have lived like an automaton who does not have to rescue a human soul in distress, who does not have to destroy evil or inspire peace or justify any purpose, like a machine in mere physical motion, obeying the laws of physics only, letting all human problems go. Like an animal—like one of my pigs!"

They laughed together. Something was released.

The invalid got up and went to the dresser and took out three of her favorite silk scarves, the oriental ones, with the patterns that reminded her of a Moorish screen or of the Arabic script in certain illuminated manuscripts.

"I want you to have something of mine," she said. "Choose the one you like best."

"You choose for me. Which one do you think will suit me best?"

She gave her friend the black one with the dark orange pattern around the edges. In Olgivanna's eyes she could see the sad knowledge that this was a parting gift. She could not bear it. She went back to the bed.

"I am very tired," she murmured. "I think I will rest now."

"I will keep it always," her friend said. "It will remind me of a strange unhappy day, a day I want never to forget."

"Olgivanna," the invalid said, as the door began to close. "You will not forget your promise to introduce me to Patrick's aunt."

"I will not forget."

15 December

Cannot get a wink of sleep. Down to the kitchen before dawn to ask for a cup of coffee. The kitchen crew is already hard at work, but Mr. Rachmilevich, a kitchen habitué, pours me a big mug, much more than I can drink, from the breakfast pot and brings me a scone hot from the oven. And he does so with such a genuine and ready smile; the negative thoughts I have toward him smite me sorely.

I take my coffee and scone into the breakfast room in order to be out of the way, but it is cold there and the empty tables make me sad. I turn back to the warmth of the kitchen and perch on a high stool in a corner. I'm cheered by the noise and the bustle of activity. Nobody seems hindered by my presence.

Enter Miss Madison. I open my mouth to bid her good morning, but she passes me with a cold look from her fish-like eye. If that's the way you want to be, my dear, say I, you may suit yourself. But suddenly she is beside me, staring down at the mug and the scone. She hopes that I will not make a habit of asking for an early breakfast. I am aware, am I not, that no one is allowed in the kitchen at this hour save the crew for the day. It is a rule that Mr. Gurdjieff is especially strict about. What would happen if every Tom, Dick, and Harry were to wander into the kitchen whenever the mood took them? Why, the efficient running of the kitchen and the prompt serving of meals would be rendered nearly impossible. We simply cannot have people getting under foot, and exasperating the cooks. She is sure that I understand. *Do* I understand? And she stands there in front of me, in her faded gown and gimcrack jewelry, insisting on my capitulation. Where is Rachmilevich, my co-conspirator? The ground has opened and swallowed him!

All of a sudden a jolt of energy runs through me. The nerve of her! She has no right to treat me this way, and she knows it. To take me to task before the entire kitchen crew, in her spindly, affected voice. After I had felt sorry for the woman, had acknowledged her humanity, had hoped that people would come to like her! As if I had ever asked for special consideration before now. If anything, I have gone out of my way to make life easy for the kitchen people, to avoid imposing upon them with my special needs, to be self-effacing and even self-sacrificing, because I feel that I am here on sufferance and that I cannot allow people to think I am a helpless invalid who requires the care of a full-time nurse...

I want to give her a piece of my mind. Do I have the right? A little voice whispers, You may do so, my girl, and have the pleasure of it, but you will lose the chance to see what is in you, to get to the bottom of it, to work on yourself—which is why you are here.

A confused struggle ensues within me. In the end I say nothing, simply bow my head. She stalks away, rigid and graceless as a stick, leaving me blushing like a girl. I deposit my coffee and half-eaten scone upon the counter and go out into the hall. Near to tears and grateful that at least there is no one about, I mount the stairs slowly and at last attain the sanctuary of my room.

I creep to my chair and stare with unseeing eyes out of the window. What is to be gained from such a struggle? What does it all mean? Isn't it simply a futile asceticism to force oneself to bite one's tongue in this manner? What is to be gained from it?

And then suddenly it comes to me, through the sunlit window, out of the air, what it means, for me, at any rate, if for no one else. It means that I still lack the inner authority that I crave, the freedom from one's own disreputable reactions. I *could* have protested against such treatment, but it would have been a protest arising out of weakness, out of irritation, rather than out of a clear perception of the situation and a sense of one's own worth. And if I had protested, I wouldn't have seen that. Now *that* is interesting, that is worth the confusion, the humiliation...

But it will not be yours, this inner authority, when it comes. You want to own it, to possess it, to make it do your bidding. It isn't like that. It is something that is above all that, above all the smoke and confusion, the rudderless turning hither and thither. It comes from a higher level of life. You must put yourself at its disposal. You must sacrifice all pettiness for it, all evasion and deception. This is hard; it feels like loss of self, loss of self-respect even. But it is what *gives* self-respect. You have to have faith in the existence of that which is higher than the impulse to wound. And then there is really no loss of self or of anything valuable, but the presence of something in you that can take command, that is worthy of respect, that can exercise authority and compassion both.

Have faith! Only then will it come...

LOVE

KM

21 December

I am sitting alone by the window in the large room with the piano, the room I was shown into on the day I arrived with Ida. Suddenly Patrick appears in the doorway and rushes toward me across the empty floor.

"Mrs. Murry! Mrs. Murry!"

"Hello, Patrick. Where have you been? I haven't seen you in a whole week."

This is not the way I wish to greet him. But I have said it before I can stop myself.

"I went to London with my aunt."

"How lovely! Did you have a nice time?"

He shakes his head impatiently, as though my question is an irrelevance.

"Mrs. Murry! I have something to tell you. You are the first person at the Prieuré to know. I haven't even told Mr. Gurdjieff."

A sudden catch at the heart. "What is it, Patrick?"

"I'm going to America—to see my father! He's sent for me! He wants me to live with him!"

"Oh, Patrick!"

"I'm going to go for Christmas, if my aunt can get tickets for the boat."

For Christmas! So soon. In the ruin of my hopes, all I can think is that I had looked forward to giving Patrick a gift, so that I could nourish the illusion of belonging to this world, the fantasy of being a mother spending Christmas with her child. But even that is to be denied me.

"What's the matter, Mrs. Murry?"

"I'm a little sad because you're leaving, Patrick."

He clamps his hand upon the crown of his head and regards me with interest.

"Don't be sad. It's not the end of the world."

In spite of myself I have to smile.

"What do you mean, Patrick?"

"I'll come back next summer, to see you and Mr. Gurdjieff. My aunt said so. Maybe my father will come too. The time won't be long in passing. It's already December."

The child is consoling me. Shouldn't I be the one to console him?

"You'll still be here, Mrs. Murry? You won't go away?"

I take a deep breath.

"If I go anywhere," I say, "it will only be for a short time. I wouldn't want to miss seeing you, Patrick."

"It's all right then," he says, as though relieved.

He seems about to dash off when he suddenly checks himself and plops down beside me on the couch. I steal a glance at him. I realize that he is aware of the impact his news has had on me. He does not want to go away immediately after delivering such news. He is going to keep me company until I feel better.

"When did you last see your father, Patrick?"

I hear the sound of my own voice as I say this. I am aware of my presence, of the strange and intimately familiar sense of being me, of this personality with its myriad needs and wants that derive from its uniquely personal history, and of the child beside me, whom I love, who is somehow connected to me, to my spent and wasted life.

"Why do you want to know?" Patrick asks.

"Because I am interested in you, Patrick," I smile back at him, "in a way that I have never been interested in any little boy before. You are my favorite of all the little boys I have ever known."

"Including your brother?"

A sharp spasm of pain. I wait for it to pass.

"Including my brother, Patrick, though I miss him very much. I'll miss you too, when you go away. I want to know about your father—so that I will be able to imagine you and him together."

Patrick considers this for a while, his face serious.

"He told me he would always be there," he says tearfully. "He came and put his arms around me. I'll never go away, he said. But he did go. My mother told me to stop crying. You're just the same as him, she said. You're just as bad."

"I'm sure she didn't really think that, Patrick."

"She did! She did!" he says excitedly. "That's what she said."

"But now you're going to see him, Patrick. Now you'll be together."

He is staring straight ahead, twin vertical lines of a frown between his eyebrows. We sit together in the failing light while the sounds of the house are borne faintly to our ears, the rattle of pans from the kitchen, footsteps overhead, a shout of laughter from the stairs.

Who knows what will become of him? Who knows what his father is like and whether Patrick will be happy with him? If only I could protect him, if only I could stand between him and the world! This must be what parents feel, what they are supposed to feel, for every child needs protection—and some of them must actually get it. It is hard for me to imagine parents who set aside their own needs for the sake of their children, but that must be the way it's supposed to be. That must be what Love is like.

"I asked my mother to come with me, to see Mr. Gurdjieff," he says suddenly, his voice raw and tearful again. "I said he was just like Granda. She said, I don't want to know anyone like Granda ever again."

He turns to me, half choked by sobs, his eyes large and pleading in the twilight.

"I cried and said Mr. Gurdjieff was a good man. She wouldn't look at me. My aunt asked her would she sign the paper and she said to me, Is that what you want? I didn't say anything. My aunt told her I wanted to see my father. Please yourself, she said. But you have no mother now, she said. I don't ever want to see you again."

He throws himself across my lap, sobbing as though his heart will break. I put my arms around him and bend over him, holding him. The force of his sobs makes me tremble.

When he grows quiet, I lean back to allow him to straighten up, but he continues to lie across my knees. Every now and then he sighs deeply. Finally he sits up. But he does not move away. He continues to sit close to me, his eyes downcast, tears gleaming faintly on his lashes. I hold out a handkerchief to him, but he does not take it. He permits me to dab his wet cheeks.

I am overcome by his confidences. I want this moment of closeness to continue indefinitely. But what can I *say* to him? "I have been talking with my grandmother, Patrick," I say. "Do you remember you told me that she would listen?"

He does not reply, but I know that I have his attention.

"I told her about my friend Patrick, who carries my chair and takes such good care of me. She is very happy that I have such a wonderful little boy for my friend. And she gave me a message for you."

He is sitting very upright, almost tense with listening. And I have the joyful sense that my love surrounds him!

"She said that if anyone is unkind to Patrick, he must remember the people who love him: his grandfather, Mr. Gurdjieff, his friends at the Prieuré. If he does this, no one will be able to hurt him. And he will grow up to be a wonderful man."

Patrick's frown has disappeared. His beautiful eyes seem clear of distress.

"My grandfather, Old Malachy, Mr. Gurdjieff," he says brightly, getting to his feet. "And Mrs. Murry."

Almost blinded by tears, I glimpse his slight form, silhouetted against the remains of the light from the windows.

"I am glad you are going to your father, Patrick," I tell him, in a quivering voice.

"I must go and tell Mr. Gurdjieff. He will be glad too."

His footsteps scampering across the floor. Sweetness and sadness commingle until I hardly know whether I am still among the living—or have I floated out of time altogether to wander the dark eternal fields of the dead?

23.XII.22
Le Prieuré

Dear Ida,

This is to wish you a happy Xmas. I have not written to you for a little while. I wanted to give you the opportunity to be "unto yourself," to live your own life without my interference, to make your own judgment about the path you have chosen for yourself. And I felt that you yourself wanted to be left alone, at bottom. I was right, wasn't I? But you have been on my mind today, and indeed all week. How are you?

There is something I would like to say to you. Promise me you will not be tragic. It does me no good for you to worry about me, Ida dear. It is as though you took my hand and began to gnaw on it. Worry is a waste of energy. It's a sin against the Light. You see this, don't you? It helps neither you nor me. And it isn't as though my existence here were miserable or empty. Au contraire! In a way it is the fullest life I have ever known...

I have not been just to you in the past. But Katie, I hear you say. No, let it stand. I have not been just. I am such an unruly little mouse, so hard to get along with. And it is more than that. There are things in me that are...simply unspeakable, the existence of which even you who know me better than anyone cannot suspect. I want to say that I am sorry for the way I have treated you, for past sins of impatience, intolerance, and worse. And I *am* sorry. I want to say too that I did not mean the things I said, that words uttered in the heat of anger or in the depths of despair must not be heeded, that I have always had a "bad character," that I am not worthy of a devotion such as yours. I do wish I had not said hurtful things, for bitter words leave their mark and there is nothing to be done about it. But I have learned since I have been here that these things are *in me* and therefore *my* responsibility, whether I like it or not, over and above any extenuating circumstances. I have learned that I must not disavow my bad character nor deny what is in me nor try to explain it away as accidental or provisional. There are so many ways to avoid seeing what one is really like. I have learned that I must acknowledge and accept myself in all of my phases and moods. This is what it means truly to have compassion, for oneself first of all and then for others. In this, Mr. Gurdjieff is an incomparable model; in his presence one senses this compassion, this acceptance of all that is bad and shameful in people, which goes beyond anything I have ever experienced...

But please do not think I am asking *you* to accept my failings. Nothing of the sort. I have been at fault in regard to you, and I ask you to forgive me. Will you? I cannot promise to change, at least not right away. The first stage is to see what is in one, to come into possession of it, to taste its bitterness to the full. Then, if one can do that, a new kind of life, a new kind of experience, may be possible. I say "may" advisedly, for if I understand what I have been told, there are no guarantees in this work. But I wanted you to know what I am engaged in, understand it in whatever way you wish. I am trying to put things to rights, to set my house in order. My debt to you is immense: I do not think it can ever be repaid. Think only of our travels, in which you were quite literally my support—without you I would have simply fallen to the ground! But that is the old life, that is our old friendship, full of frights and wrecks and misunderstandings. When I am well, when I have learned all this place has to teach me, I shall still need a friend. If you'd like me for a friend—a *new* friend—as from this Xmas, I'd like to be your friend. But not too awfully serious, *ma chère*. Perhaps I shall leave here shortly and set up in a little farm in the South and keep some animals and grow things. Come with me if you promise to smile now and then. *Dear* Ida! The tragic mood is not for the likes of us. We are never more ridiculous than when we are mournful...

Write and tell me of life on your farm. Do you massage your cows after they have given birth? How is your stable kept? What is the condition of the floor?

And remember, Ida dear: In spite of what I have said—and shall say—you have been a 'perfect' friend to me.

Yours ever
KM

23.XII.22
Le Prieuré

Darling Bogey,

Just a note to wish you a Happy Xmas. I wonder very much how you who always say you hate Xmas so will spend it this year. Perhaps the Dunning family will make it seem real. Do tell me how you get along.

We are going to *fêter le Noel* in tremendous style here. Up until the other day I was under the impression that the chief cele-bration would take place on the Russian Christmas, which is not for another fortnight. But Mr. Gurdjieff announced that the English are to have a celebration of their own, in the traditional, old-fashioned English manner. There are only a handful of them, but that makes no difference to his idea of hospitality. The Russians are to be our guests, and we shall sit down to table sixty strong—to a whole sheep, a pig, two turkeys, a goose, wine by the barrel, and an enormous pudding made in a baby's bathtub, stirred by everybody in the community, containing a coin tossed in by Mr. Gurdjieff that entitles the lucky finder to receive our new-born calf as a present. Would that this darling little creature were mine! I was there at his birth. He was pulled unceremoniously from his mother by a rope tied about his leg which he did not seem to mind. And there is an immense tree in the salon, lavishly decorated with paper flowers were made by the younger children under the direction of yours truly; the children are beside themselves at the prospect of gifts from Father Xmas. There is to be music and reading, and Mr. Salzmann has persuaded me to read something from Shakespeare. I am considering Bottom's scenes in A *Midsummer's Night's Dream*; many of the Russians do not understand English, much less Shakespeare, but they may be entertained by my accent. And perhaps one of the little girls can be persuaded to play Peaseblossom.

I attended the obsequies of the pig this morning. Since I am going to feast on him, I thought it was the least I could do. Yesterday I watched Madame Ostrowska pluck, singe, and draw our birds. These are gory days. I take refuge in the salon—with the fairy-like tree. I am truly grateful to be here. One feels so much more the meaning of Christmas when one's life is merged with that of the community.

This is not a letter, only a note scribbled on a table piled with paper flowers, gold wire, gilded fir cones. God bless you darling.

Ever your
Wig

24 December ·

After all the festivities—Mr. Gurdjieff as a jolly patriarch, Rachmilevich as Father Xmas! the children gathered around me, listening with such rapt attention to words they could not under-stand—I came away early, having eaten no more than a pick. I had commissioned Orage to find a gift for me to give to Patrick (who is with us for another week), but he had been unable to go to Par-is and returned from Avon with a box of pencils, which looked so very meager that I was almost ashamed to put it under the tree. Never mind: Patrick received his share of gifts. I looked for him to say goodnight and to wish him a Happy Xmas, but we were sepa-rated at table and I had to be content to wave to him across the boisterous room. I went up to my room alone, feeling thoroughly exhausted, and a little frightened.

But a surprise awaited me. When I opened my door, there was a cheerful fire on the hearth and to one side a small bushy Christmas tree adorned with three lighted candles. And Adèle, standing by the window, her eyes shining.

"This is our little tree, just for the two of us," she said. "And nobody shall know about it."

"But Adèle, why three candles?"

She led me to the armchair and draped my blue and white scarf about my shoulders. She moved up a footstool and placed herself on the floor beside me.

"One for myself," she murmured, "and one for Mrs. Murry. And there must be a third for the one of whom she always thinks, whose letters she awaits with such impatience."

She smiled up at me.

"You look so lovely tonight," she said.

And it was true that I had dressed with special care, wearing my dark purple taffeta with the shoulder straps and the tiny embroi-dered flowers, and brushing my hair back from my forehead, a new style for me. But I was sad. What is the use of looking lovely if...?

We sat in silence, looking at our Christmas tree.

"I am *so* sorry, Mrs. Murry. But he is going to his father. And you will find another..."

One of the candles flickered and began to go out. I could not help myself.

"That's me," I whispered.

"No! no!" she exclaimed, and jumping up she put out the others first. Then she threw herself down again, embraced my knees, and rested her forehead against me. I could tell that she was making a great effort to hold back her tears.

"I'm sorry," I said. "It's a silly superstition. If a candle goes out, a soul goes to heaven."

"It is where you belong," she sobbed. "You are too good for this world."

I had to smile.

"Would that I were."

She raised her head. Her cheeks were tear-stained, but she had finished weeping.

"Do you want to know what my grandmother told me? God makes his specially chosen ones to suffer much, but only to bind them to Him more closely, to make them His own."

"Do you think I am one of God's own?"

"I know it," she said.

There was such a look of trusting confidence in her young open face that I could have believed it.

"May it be so," I said. "I am tired tonight. It must be the excitement."

She got up immediately, placed a hot water bottle in my bed, and kissed me shyly on the cheek.

"I wish I could meet your husband," she said. "He must be a wonderful person."

I felt a strange fluttering sensation at my heart, a sense of alarm that was momentarily acute and then passed, leaving an unexpected calm in its wake, the calm of decision.

"You *will* meet him. I am going to invite him to come here for the opening of our Study House. I will ask Mr. Gurdjieff tomorrow."

She gave a little jump of excitement.

"And I will introduce you as a very special friend."

"Happy Christmas, Mrs. Murry," she said, blushing with pleasure. "Sleep well."

25 December

Sitting by the window in the salon looking out at the frosty lawns while behind me a huge fire roars up the chimney. To me Rachmilevich, drawing up a chair. A sinking feeling: how to extra-cate myself, how to get rid of him. His smile is one of complicity; we understand each other, it says; we are two of a kind. Is there anything he can do for Mrs. Merry? I shake my head mutely. There is something I can do for him though, and that is why he is here. I can listen to him complain. He is treated poorly, is Rachmilevich, and no one has any sympathy for him. Why, only the other day he found a lump of coke in his soup. A lump of coke! How did it happen that a lump of coke turned up in Rachmilevich's bowl and in no one else's? It was Patrick who served the soup. Now do I understand? And everyone else pretended not to notice. Georgivanich insisted that it was the best soup he had ever tasted. He even claimed that from now on a lump of coke should be added to the recipe since it so greatly improved the taste. But it was all in order to humiliate Rachmilevich. Nobody has the slightest consideration for him. And this is supposed to be a place dedicated to Christian charity and love of one's neighbor. Did I want to know what he thought? There is no more of Christian charity in most of the people here than in—a Turk! And as for Georgivanich. He has known Georgivanich for a very long time, and if only his lips were not sealed... And as for those awful children...

He bends over me, in his shabby clothes, his breath smelling of tobacco. He is my friend now, and I loathe his familiarity, but I smile and smile and eventually he goes away.

Yes, it is the old thing returning upon me with renewed force, my instinctive hatred of people, if they are not the "right" sort of people, if they lack the right "sensitivity," if they do not share my feelings about literature and fine things and table manners and teacups—oh! I am simply appalled by my helplessness. The only way is to court this helplessness, to face it, not to turn away. But what a relief when Rachmilevich finally leaves me in peace!

Later—with a sort of thunderclap!—while sitting in my room thinking of nothing: I know why I dislike Rachmilevich so much! It is because we *are* alike, he and I, not only in being members of the same species, but in the much more particular sense of—being complainers. Rachmilevich is simply more honest: he does not make any bones about his disaffection with humanity, whereas I am always trying to couch my complaints in reasonable terms. At bottom, it comes to the same thing; I am not satisfied with things, with people, with what I have and have not, and I wish to express my dissatisfaction. I resent it when other people complain about *their* lives because I know that the amount of sympathy available to complainers is a finite quantity.

I sit as if stunned. Exquisite pain. I do not want to believe it. I would give anything not to have to do so. But the moment in which I could have turned aside is past. What is it like, this merciless seeing? It is like walking into a room in which two guilty lovers embrace. You try frantically to get out, but the door has closed behind you. You fumble for the door handle, but all the while you cannot help but see *what is there.*

And then, just when I think I can no longer stand it, just when my little bark is about to be overwhelmed—the incredible calm in the eye of the storm. *This is what I am like.* And what a relief it is to finally stop pretending, to lay down one's arms, to cease to support this futile and disreputable cause. What a sense of—freedom!

26 December

I did not sleep. But it was not fear or unhappiness that kept me awake. All night I felt a presence in the room—my own! I was filled with an inexplicable joy. I did not wish to close my eyes for fear I would miss a moment of it.

Finally I got up and sat at my table in the first light of day. I intended to write something about what I was feeling, but when Olgivanna came in an hour later I had still not picked up my pencil. She was wearing the scarf I had given her, and she looked the picture of loveliness.

"How is everything this morning?" she asked gaily.

"I feel—wonderful! This place has worked a kind of miracle for me."

"And you have been here barely two months."

"Two months? Two thousand years, you mean!"

She laughed happily.

"Yes," she said. "We have only been friends for two months. But I feel I have known you for a long time."

"Thousands of years—if all were told! You and I are *old* friends, Olgivanna. Much older than we know."

The smile faded from her face as I watched her, and I was afraid that she was going to cry. I bowed my head over the desk. I remembered how as a child I had asked my grandma to promise me that she would never die. She would not promise. Her gentle face assumed a sad, almost stern expression that frightened me and made me plead with her: Promise me, my grandma. She would not.

I felt the features of my face take on the same expression. I was sure that I looked like her as I sat there. I picked up my pencil and began to doodle in the corner of my page, a little doodle of a scarab beetle that my grandmother liked to make, her special emblem.

"But Olgivanna, sometimes I have my doubts. Will you tell me the truth? Do you still believe I am on the right way?"

"I certainly do. That is what your happiness is telling you."

"What if I tell you that all my old feelings, habits, and desires have returned upon me with redoubled force? My hatred, my intolerance, my instinctive hostility to people. All the faults and failings of my old life that only a month ago I repudiated as worthless, that I thought to rid myself of as a snake sheds an old skin. I am still attached to them all. And to Monsieur Self-Love and Madame Vanity! What if even my very clothes—and the clothes that one dear to me is wearing—are precious to my eyes and touch? What then? Would you still believe I am on the right way?"

She came and sat opposite me with her back to the window, her hands resting in her lap.

"Yes, you are on the right way," she said with quiet conviction. "Those old feelings and desires will always be there; you cannot simply chop them off like the branch of a dead tree. But they return to you made precious by your work; through them you have made a new life. Do you not remember what you told me when you first came here? I have lived a false life, and I no longer believe in it. Well, you have courageously destroyed that life and built yourself a new one. I rejoice for you."

My heart was beating with an excitement I could hardly contain.

"If I have done all you say, how is it I do not know it for myself? But it makes me very happy to hear what you have said."

Someone called for Olgivanna in the corridor. She got up hastily. I got up too and took her hands.

"I will come this evening," she said.

"Only if you are not too tired. But there is one thing I must ask you before you go. My husband is coming next week. He will not know me with my hair like this. Do you think it will seem very foolish if I comb my bangs down again?"

Her face relaxed, and her sweet smile returned.

"That is the way you wore your hair when I first saw you at breakfast with the English," she said. "When you first touched my heart."

A swift pressure of her fingers, and she was gone.

1 January

The New Year is already here. I must leave the fire and go to bed. No Christmas or New Year's message from my father. Perfunctory greetings from my sisters, relayed through Jack; for some reason they are unable to believe that I can receive mail here.

No matter. All goes away: Grandma, Chummie, Mother, Patrick. It is the law that we are under.

God bless you, Darling Father. May we meet again.

2 January

Unable to sleep. Great agitation of mind. I come downstairs in the dead of night, my heart pounding, and make my way into the kitchen where a night light is burning and I realize that there is nothing I want. The thought of food makes me nauseous; I do not even want coffee. The small urgent pleasures, cigarettes and coffee and the like, have been taken from me one by one. There is nothing I want—only to be released!

A faint glow from the doorway of the salon. The fire is still burning. I go in and approach it. Suddenly I realize there is someone in the room: Mr. Gurdjieff sitting to one side, the dark bulk of him solid and motionless in his chair. I start to back out. But he raises his head, smiles his wonderful smile, and waves me into the chair beside him.

"I could not sleep, Mr. Gurdjieff."

"Ah," he murmurs. "Some people sleep at night"—as though it were a most extraordinary thing!—"Never stay up to ask, Where is God now? But we are awake. Must keep watch then. Make vigil."

At once I feel an extraordinary sense of peace and contentment. We sit in silence for a long time. I find myself listening to the sound of Mr. Gurdjieff's breathing, with which my own seems to harmonize. The fire burns down.

"When your husband come?"

"On the 9th, Mr. Gurdjieff. In time for the opening of the Study House."

He is silent again. I have the impression that he is not interested in Jack, which in a way is fair since Jack is not interested in him. But it saddens me all the same. I want Jack to share in this experience with me, if only a little. But perhaps he will.

"You want to ask me something?"

I can see him only faintly, his shaven head gleaming redly in the light from the embers.

"If it is true that I do not have a soul," I begin, "if it is true that I must make one by my own efforts—"

"Is true!"

"Then what am I to do?"

"You must help your mother."

For a moment I think I have not heard correctly.

"My mother is dead, Mr. Gurdjieff."

"I know. You tell already. But you *are* your mother. Because of your mother—and father—you are here. There is a debt of gratitude between you. Gratitude is a sacred emotion, not like other emotions. Your mother is dead. Too late for her to mend her life. You must mend for her. Help her."

Something in me revolts against what he is telling me. I do not want to receive it. In my sudden anguish I cry out:

"But *how*, Mr. Gurdjieff?"

He puts his hand up to his forehead and is silent. I wait, motionless in my chair. I feel something approaching me, and I am trying with all my force to hold it at bay.

"You know what means consciousness?"

"Why, it means to know something."

"Not to know *something*," he says. "To know self. Before you come to me you not know your own 'I' for one second in your whole life. But then I tell and you try. You remember to say 'I am' sometimes?"

"I have not remembered, Mr. Gurdjieff," I say, feeling my tears begin to gather, glad of the dim light that prevents him from seeing me.

"Say once every hour. Is very difficult. You not succeed, but no matter. You try."

"How long must I do it for?"

"How long?" he exclaims. "Forever! Until no longer necessary." Then, gently: "You understand? Will help. Will make easier to bear."

He is looking at me. There is just enough light for me to see his eyes. It is not like looking at another human being at all. There is nothing of himself in his eyes, nothing of the desire to please and the secret suspicions or resentments that lurk in the gaze of every other person I have met. Nothing but his essential humanity: the gift of his attention and his unconditional compassion.

He rises, passes in front of the fire, and is gone. But something remains, a seed, growing within me, in spite of me, something long prepared in darkness, reaching now for light and air, pushing like a green seedling through the thawing earth.

The fire is extinguished. Darkness that is not quite complete, that somehow anticipates day. I pass in and out of sleep, all the time attending to an inner conversation, a Babel of voices, urging, protesting, lamenting.

At last there is a single voice, calm and clear, speaking slowly and with great deliberation.

Your parents. You have always felt tremendously at fault before them, aware only of their oft-expressed disappointment in you. But what about *your* disappointment in them? For you *are* disappointed in them, are you not? And you do not wish to acknowledge this. Why? Because to acknowledge your disappointment would require you to give up your cherished illusion of family, your hope of finding refuge and sustenance in a barren place. It would bring home to you as never before that this is what you get in life, this—and no more. You see it out of the corner of your eye, even if you can't quite look it full in the face. This is what you get. This is *all* you get. You feel very sad about this, very sorry for yourself. You pass this way only one time, and you will never know what it is like to have a loving mother, a father who is interested in you, sisters with whom you share what is closest to your heart. It can never be. You have been given a great deal to make up for this loss—Granny Dyer and Chummie and Ida and all of the years with Jack, and Orage and even Lawrence, in spite of all. Mr. Gurdjieff and Olgivanna and Adèle. And Patrick. But it is a deep unhealed wound nonetheless, part of the truly inescapable suffering of this world, and something that must be faced...

I know now what Mr. Gurdjieff was telling me about my mother, and I no longer have to keep it at arms' length. My mother left me no share of her great fortune because she thought I had disgraced the family and married beneath myself. All the same, a kind of legacy came down to me. My mother did not love her children. I suppose she loved them as much as it was in her to love. But it was not enough. And she turned on me in my hour of need with a vindictiveness that still surprises me. That is what Gurdieff meant when he said, You are your mother. She has bequeathed to me her indifference, her coldness, her bitter tongue, her fear of love and tenderness. This bequest must go no further. This is my work, the work for which I have been given breath. God send that I be spared to do it, if only for a little while...

4 January 1923

Patrick is to leave today. All morning I have been dreading the farewell. I do not know whether to go downstairs or to wait for him to come to me. In the end I decide that it will be harder for me to say goodbye to him if there are others present. But what if he does not come?

At noon, just when I am about to go in search of him, I hear his step in the hall, his familiar knock.

"It's my birthday," he announces.

"A happy birthday, Patrick. May it be your best ever."

He pats the crown of his head, saunters over to the window, and looks out.

"What are you doing today, Mrs. Murry?"

"I believe I will stay indoors, Patrick. How the wind blows outside. It will be too cold for me."

He sprawls on the window seat, looking bored. I watch him from the bed.

"My aunt is here," he says. "She is going to take me on the boat."

"You must be excited."

He shrugs.

"Or maybe you are just a little bit afraid?" I tease, hoping to introduce some levity into the proceedings.

He ponders this seriously.

"No," he decides. "But Mrs. Murry—"

"Yes, Patrick."

"Do you think I will still be able to talk to my grandfather when I am in America?"

"I don't see why not."

"How will he know where I am? Isn't it a long way?"

"It *is* a long way, Patrick. But it is a very big boat. There is plenty of room for a stowaway."

He does not seem reassured. He toys with the fringe of a cushion.

"I wish *you* were coming with me, Mrs. Murry."

My throat is constricted, and I cannot reply. I sit up and swing my legs onto the floor. I want to go to him, but I am afraid that an expression of emotion will upset him.

"Listen to me, Patrick. Your grandfather will always be with you. Do you know why? Because he is inside of you, just the way my grandma is inside of me. You can talk to him any time you want. All you have to do is to remember that he is there."

His eyes widen in amazement. Such love I feel for him in this moment.

"It's true!" I say. "And let me tell you something else."

"What?"

"I have been talking with my grandma again."

"What did she say?" he murmurs.

"She said I am going home."

"To New Zealand?"

I nod, pressing my lips together to stop their trembling.

"I am going home too," he says.

"That's right, Patrick," I say, trying to smile.

"I *am* a little bit afraid. What if he doesn't like me?"

"Everyone likes you, Patrick. Your father will like you too, when he gets to know you."

My heart is full of love for him. He *is* my little boy, the only one I will ever have. I know that he will miss me, that I have been a significant person in his life, call it parent or aunt or friend—or godmother. But there is no time save the present in which to savor this knowledge.

"You will be able to talk to me too, Patrick, if you like."

"What do you mean, Mrs. Murry?"

"I mean that I will always be with you, Patrick," I stammer. "In my heart."

It is not the sort of thing you say to a child. He considers it gravely. Has he guessed what I cannot tell him?

"You must write too," he says. "Because you are a writer, aren't you?"

"Yes, Patrick," I say, the laughter coming unexpectedly to my lips. "That is what I am."

He rises suddenly.

"Well, Mrs. Murry," he says, with a comically adult formality. "It's time."

"I want to give you something, Patrick. For your birthday. It is on the dresser"

He walks over to the dresser and picks up my grandmother's brass pig.

"Pigs never see the stars," he remarks.

"Mr. Gurdjieff?"

We chuckle together.

"This is a very special pig," I tell him. It used to belong to my grandmother, and at times I think that there is something of her in it. I would like you to have it."

"Is there something of *you* in it, Mrs. Murry?

"I suppose there is, Patrick."

"Then I'll use it as a telephone," he says, grinning. "When I want to hear from you, I'll hold it up to my ear."

Shouts in the corridor: Patrick! Patrick Miller! He thrusts the pig into his pocket and rushes for the door. I make a grab for him as he passes. A hug to which, surprisingly, he yields himself quietly—until I let him go.

"God bless, Patrick."

The door standing open, facing the blank wall of the corridor. The sound of rapid footsteps on the stairs, receding. The winter light coming in at the window, gilding the dresser with its little bright spot of absence where stood my grandma's pig...

This was the hardest thing. Whatever is to come cannot be harder.

5 January

"My dear friend," I said to Orage. "I have found my idea. I have got it at last. Your Katya has felt something that she never felt in her life before...

"When my brother died, it was a very great blow to me. It seemed he could not possibly be dead, he who was so alive, who was everywhere, within me and around me. We had been almost like one child, as though we saw the world through the same eyes, touched it with the same hands. And when he died, I thought I had lost my fear of death, because I was already dead, just as much dead as he, though I still walked upright upon the earth and he was lying in the middle of a little wood in France. There remained only to write of the time we had shared, the time of our lives, to put down my recollections of New Zealand, to discharge a sacred debt to my own country because he and I were born there. Thus we might still be at one, ranging together over all the remembered places of our childhood. I would write it—then I should be with him.

"But instead I wrote about what it was like to be a child in our family—what it was like for me. It is not that I shouldn't have written as I did; after all, I did observe those things, and I had to set them down. But my attitude toward them was all wrong. It was a partial and misleading attitude and not a little malicious, and it determined the taste of my stories, as it were. Look, it said, here is what families are like, what is there to do about it? And my stories had no other purpose that to record this attitude, to parade it before people, to seek their approval of it. When it was this attitude that stood most in need of change."

"Now I want to live, and I have set a new goal in my writing that will be consonant with life. Chekhov reproached himself for lacking such a goal. He felt that with the best of writers each line is saturated with the consciousness of the goal, one feels life as it should be in addition to life as it is and one is captivated by it. And yet that is just what is immanent in his stories: life as it should be, lurking behind or above the disreputable facade of life as it is...

"No one who wants for nothing, Chekhov said, who hopes for nothing and who fears nothing—can be an artist. Very well. What is it that I want? I want to imbue my work with the sense of our possibilities as human beings—rather than, as in the case of the old KM, to bring a passive, secretly resentful attitude to bear upon my tale. I have buried the old writer in me, and the world will no longer be subjected to her tedious and self-justifying manner. I hope to write one story, if only one, that I would dare to show to God. And I fear only the consequences of betraying this goal, of lying to myself and my readers, of failing to live up to all that I know...

"My book, the book I am obliged now to write, is a book of the dead, of *my* dead, which I must write as one living—with pity and understanding and forgiveness for all, and most especially for the child I was..."

8 January

A dream. Early morning, mist burning off over Day's Bay, exquisitely scented air, and silence, pure and sacred silence, broken only by the sleepy murmur of the sea. I am walking above the rocks at Downes Point. It is my beloved bay, that I have longed for so deeply of late, but changed, nay, transfigured, by a golden autumnal foliage, the brilliant colors of dying leaves, a more dramatic fall than dear New Zealand has ever seen—and pervading all, a powerful feeling of joy. I walk with a spring in my step, with never a care for shortness of breath or the hectic beating of my heart, my arms raised above my head in sheer exultation. Why am I so happy? I am on the Way.

The scene changes. I encounter a dog (Philos?) who takes my hand in his mouth, but gently, to lead me. A height above the sea: I know it is still NZ, but I do not recognize it. The light is strange, like a photographic negative, and it begins to snow, black snow from a black sky. Philos leads me on. I am afraid, I know I should turn back. What if something should happen to my guide?

The fear of falling over a precipice, of lying down exhausted in the snow to die. But I press on in spite of my fear. After all, I am on the Way!

Another change of scene: the golden road again, through the blazing leaves. A sense of excitement and expectation, I am on my way to meet someone I dearly love. Is it my grandmother? Is it Chummie? Patrick? Is it Jack? I am breathing rapidly as though I have been running. My heart is beating madly in my chest. At any moment now I will turn the last corner and see the beloved face...

I awake and lie there blissfully, entirely free of pain, a corona of love still diffused about me. And now I know that whatever comes, there is something in me that will be able to meet it, gently, with compassion and acceptance. To cease from futile struggle. To perceive the illusion of separateness. To know myself to be part of a greater whole.

I am home. I know my way. Out of this world I cannot fall.

LM

On the evening of 9th January, 1923, Katherine was taken
from us. The following day I received a telegram in Lisieux from Murry and caught the afternoon train.

I had seen Katherine for the last time at Fontainebleau on
20th October. I felt terribly ill at ease at the Priory, though everyone there had been kind. I could not remain, however much I
feared for Katherine. And indeed I was aware that she did not
wish me to. My reason told me that she would be adequately
looked after, but my heart was full of foreboding, and I came away
in a sort of daze.

I returned to Paris and sat down in Katherine's old room at
the Rue de la Sorbonne. How little of me was left after my separation from Katherine! She had seemed happy at the Priory, as
though she were embarking upon a great adventure, and I was
happy for her, and relieved for myself, since I was no longer subject to the strain of trying to *make* her happy. But that strain had
been at the center of my life for so long that its absence made me
feel like an empty shell. It was my own fault that such an attachment had developed, as Katherine herself had often told me. I
determined now to take advantage of circumstances and create a
life of my own, which I would have lacked the will to do had the
task not been thrust upon me.

I went to work at a farm near Lisieux, because I felt happier
with animals and simple people. But I still suffered from what
Katherine called "toothache," a gnawing sense of helplessness and
distress. Katherine felt that it was no more than growing pains;
when I had established myself in a new life independent of hers I
would no longer suffer from it. When I had built for myself a boat
of my own—to use Katherine's metaphor—in which to sail upon the
River of Life, then a new relationship would be established between
us, and we would be able to sail together without sacrificing our
independence. But I knew myself that this toothache was a presen-

timent that our relationship was at an end. I was inwardly convinced that I would never again see her in life, and so the summons
to Fontainebleau, though a great blow, did not come as a surprise.

A friend of Katherine's, Olga Ivanovna, came to speak with
me shortly after I arrived at the Priory for the funeral. She was a
beautiful young woman, and I could tell that she had loved Katherine very much. She told me that Katherine had achieved the aim
that had brought her to the Priory and that for one such as she,
death was not the end, but rather a beginning. I was distraught
and could understand little. But I was happy to learn that on the
evening of her death Katherine had appeared transformed. Her
face shining with inexpressible beauty and love, she had listened
to the sacred music, and when she left the hall with Murry, she
was so filled with joy that she attempted to run up the stairs, as a
healthy person might have done. This effort made her cough and
started the fatal hemorrhage.

I was taken to the small chapel where Katherine lay in her
coffin. The room was cold and bare, and so I fetched her embroi-
dered Spanish shawl and covered her with it. I felt she would have
appreciated that. At the graveside the following day, Jack and I
stood side by side as chief mourners. Someone suggested that the
shawl should be cast into the grave. But it was a beautiful thing,
and I knew she would not want that. I looked to Murry, but he
seemed hardly to be aware of what was going on around him. So I
threw down one of the little twists of paper containing raisins,
corn, and honey that Gurdjieff had handed to the mourners. I
thought it a strange custom, but I learned afterwards that it sym-
bolized germination and re-birth.

I visited the balcony in the cow byre where Katherine had
lain and saw the wonderful paintings she had written to me about.
I walked for a long time in the garden with Mr. Orage, neither of
us speaking a word. I felt an attachment to him because he had
been kind to Katherine, and I think he understood this.

Before I left I spoke with Adèle, a young Lithuanian girl
who had been devoted to Katherine. Murry had given her some of
Katherine's clothes, including the gown she had worn to the
Christmas celebrations, and Katherine's favorite ring, a cluster of
rubies. Adèle told me how as she was carrying these clothes along
one of the upper corridors to her room in the old monks' quar-

ters, a little red-breasted bird flew in at the window, circled about her head, and fluttered out again. Her grandmother had told her that the souls of those we have loved revisit us in the form of birds. She knew by this that Katherine was at peace.

Once at Sierre Katherine said she was convinced that she would die before I did and if it came to pass she would send me a earth worm in a matchbox, as a sign that all was well with her. Not an earth worm, I protested. An earwig then, said Katherine. About a month after her death, when I was fearfully downcast, I arrived at a small cottage in the country to assist Jack with her papers. There was ill feeling between us at the time because he was going to publish her journals and I knew that Katherine had instructed him to burn as much as possible, to make a clean sweep of her camping ground, as she put it. I wished to make a cup of tea to cheer myself a little, and I reached for a matchbox to light the gas. It seemed empty—but something rattled inside. When I opened it, there was Katherine's earwig. I could not help smiling.

One evening not long afterwards, as I was working with Murry, I felt that she came into the room. She passed by me, smiling, and continued on her way. Murry lifted his head and said, "You have seen Katherine." I think he was sad that he had not seen her himself.

Her face was radiant, as though she walked in sunlight, and my spirits were lifted at last.